To Heath... Keep ... ...

hashbrown Winters

and the

Phantom of Pordunce

Frank L. Cole

Bonneville Books
Springville, Utah

More books by Frank L. Cole

The Adventures of Hashbrown Winters
Hashbrown Winters and the Mashimoto Madness
The Guardians of the Tebah Stick (coming March 2011)

© 2010 Frank L. Cole
All rights reserved.

ISBN 13: 978-1-59955-398-6

Published by Bonneville Books, an imprint of Cedar Fort, Inc., 2373 W. 700 S., Springville, UT 84663
Distributed by Cedar Fort, Inc., www.cedarfort.com

LIBRARY OF CONGRESS CATALOGING-IN-PUBLICATION DATA
Cole, Frank, 1977-
  Hashbrown Winters and the phantom of Pordunce / Frank Cole.
     p. cm.
  Summary: A phantom is haunting the halls of Pordunce Elementary, and it is up to Hashbrown and his classmates to stop it.
  ISBN 978-1-59955-398-6
  1. Ghost stories. 2. Humorous stories. [1. Schools--Fiction. 2. Ghosts--Fiction. 3. Oracles--Fiction. 4. Humorous stories.] I. Title.

  PZ7.C673435Hax 2010
  [Fic]--dc22
                              2010024784
Cover illustration by Adam Record
Cover design by Angela Olsen
Interior illustrations and map by Tanya Quinlan
Cover design © 2010 by Lyle Mortimer
Edited and typeset by Heidi Doxey

Printed in the United States of America
10 9 8 7 6 5 4 3 2 1

Printed on acid-free paper

For Eric, Chris, Andy, and Josh—
the original members of my treehouse club.

Praise for *The Adventures of Hashbrown Winters*

Hashbrown, Snow Cone, Four Hips, Whiz, and the rest of his friends will have you laughing out loud. Frank L. Cole has created a wonderfully funny story with enough twists and turns to keep children and adults glued to their seats.

J. Scott Savage,
author of the Farworld series

An excellent book. You'll be laughing a lot as you sit on the edge of your seat. Highly recommended.

James Dashner,
author of The 13th Reality series

Praise for *Hashbrown Winters and the Mashimoto Madness*

Hashbrown Winters and the Mashimoto Madness is one enjoyable adventure. So good in fact I almost overlooked what a master Frank is with using capital letters at the start of each sentence. You're going to love this book.

Obert Skye,
author of the Leven Thumps series

Filled with crazy, hare-brained, witty humor that just sort of reaches from out of nowhere and smacks you right in the face when you're least expecting it! It will have you smiling, wincing, laughing, and downright snorting out loud before you are finished.

Phillip J. Chipping,
CEO, www.knowonder.com

Acknowledgments

It would seem that since not a whole lot of time has passed since the first Hashbrown was released, my acknowledgements wouldn't change much. Indeed, the same people who gave me encouragement and had excitement for these books in the past have not changed and are still here as my supporting cast. If it weren't for the involvement of my family, especially my wife, Heidi, Hashbrown would have never made it to the fifth grade.

Still, there are so many more amazing people I need to add to the list. To the wonderful crews at Barnes and Noble: Brandi, Michelle, Rachel, Melyn, and Angie. You beautiful people! I owe a large chunk of my success to you. To Rhonda, Deanna, Melanie, Debbie, Jared, and the rest of the Battleship crew, thank you for believing in me and humoring me with your canned laughter. Come on, my jokes aren't always that bad.

I want to give a special thanks to Kaitlyn Larkin from Sunrise Elementary, winner of the Hashbrown Winters Create-a-Character Contest. Nathanial "Nugget" Nottingham was pure genius and nothing less. I love how adding him into the mix created new ideas and characters for Hashbrown. Kaitlyn your creativity and imagination are inspiring, and I hope you love Nugget's role in *Hashbrown Winters and the Phantom of Pordunce*. I also want to thank the other 2,000+ kids that dug deep and came up with some of the most hilarious characters I have ever seen. I can't wait to read your own stories. They're bound to be hits!

As always, I need to thank Cedar Fort. Lyle, Lee, and Jennifer, where would I be without you? Thanks to Heidi, my awesome editor, and to Sheralyn . . . I'm such a fan! Heck, I'll even thank Sebi. I'm grateful for Adam Record who, as always, blew me away with his awesome illustrations.

To the members of my original writing group, Steve, Mike, and Kevin, thank you for the brainstorming sessions. I eagerly wait to read your next novels.

Last, I want to say thank you to the sweet, elderly lady who stopped me one day at a bookstore to tell me she didn't like Hashbrown Winters because there was just too much mischief. Could there have ever been a better endorsement? I think not!

Contents

Chapter 1

Terror Awakens

Deep beneath Pordunce Elementary, something trouble-some was brewing. None of the teachers or students had any idea what was happening. They had all gone home for the evening. Even Ms. Borfish sat in her trailer, watching the Home Shopping Network and laughing hysterically. They were selling peat moss—her favorite episode.

Down under the floors, below the cafeteria where the leftover tuna casserole rotted in plastic tubs, something was moving. Two somethings. Pepper and Siegfried were on the roll.

"Get back here you varmints!" Twinkles shouted. He spun around and clacked his tap shoes together. Siegfried and Pepper were two of Twinkles's hamsters, and they were rolling amok in their plastic balls. Down the narrow hallway they ran, smacking into each other.

What was wrong with them anyway? It was almost as if the hamsters were driven by some mystical force. Up ahead, Siegfried and Pepper arrived at the fork in the pathway and Twinkles stopped, resting his hand against the stone walls. The hamsters paused briefly and then shot off to the right. Twinkles smiled. They had chosen a dead end. There was nothing but a rock wall down that path. A crash rang out as the two balls collided with the wall. The chase had ended.

Twinkles scooped up his pets. "I told ya. You can't outrun me. Next time, you'd best . . ." His voice trailed off as something caught his ear. Cocking his head to the side, he listened. The sound was high-pitched, like a whistling, and it drove the hamsters crazy. They scampered, trying to charge out of Twinkles's grip.

Twinkles leaned forward, noticing a crack in the wall that started in the spot where his hamsters had plowed into it and splintered all the way to the top. He ran his fingers along the crack and then hopped back in alarm as the rock began crumbling. Chunks toppled to the ground as the crack grew larger.

Suddenly, a glowing red light flashed from the other side. More rock fell as the crack widened and the light filled the hallway.

"What have you done, boys?" Twinkles whispered.

The hole grew big enough to walk through. Twinkles felt he should leave, but his curiosity kept him glued to the spot. What could be hiding in there? He had lived most of his life down beneath Pordunce. Up until now, there had been a wall at the end of this path. He took a step toward the light, when something that shouldn't have been there appeared on the other end.

Twinkles gasped and dropped his hamsters. They immediately shot toward the opening.

"Siegfried! Pepper! No!" he shouted. But it was too late—they vanished into the glow. Suddenly a figure stepped out through the hole. Twinkles took one look at it, collapsed to the floor, threw his head back, and screamed. Siegfried and Pepper had awoken something from the other side.

Chapter 2

Bubblegum's Bad News

It couldn't have been a more perfect Wednesday. Three months of snow were over, with nothing but clear skies ahead. Not only did Groundhog Brummer not see his shadow last week, but that furry fourth grader guaranteed swimming weather by the end of March. Ms. Borfish had called off sick due to some mole infection, and the substitute lunch lady accidentally burned fifty trays of hash browns. To top it off, Principal Herringtoe decided to extend recess for an extra hour due to some termite issues. Things were definitely looking up. Snow Cone Jones and I gathered our gear and headed for the marble arena.

"Can you believe this day?" I asked, rolling my shoulders and pulling out my brand new bull basher. It was a radiant blue with white streaks swirling through it like the eye of a hurricane. Frosty John and Frankie Folds sent me the bull basher as a gift shortly after their return to Pordatraz. They were a couple of inmates at the playground prison, but they became my friends after we saved everyone in the school from turning into mindless zombies a few months ago. This new bull basher was as good as my last one, may it rest in peace somewhere in the witness relocation program.

"Yeah, it seems too good to be true," Snow Cone said, pulling out his own collection of silver shooters and buffing them with a napkin.

As we tromped past the crooked balance beam, Pigeon Criggle appeared frantically fluttering in front of us.

"Mr. Brown!" he chirped, twirling in circles. "We have a problem!"

I reared back as Pigeon's flailing arms nearly knocked my bull basher out of my hand. "Pigeon, what are you doing?"

"I'm sorry, Mr. Brown, but there's a big, nasty problem."

"What's the problem?" Snow Cone asked, looking sideways at me and rolling his eyes. Pigeon's a member of my club, but he gets overly excited about silly things.

Pigeon pressed his lips together. "It's the first graders, sir. It's . . . terrible!"

"What's wrong with them?" I asked.

"Razor Cannelloni told them there's gold hiding in the sandbox. Now, they're over there digging through it with a flour sifter. It's not pretty!"

"Yikes!" The sandbox was off-limits to everyone except Ms. Borfish's cats. Believe me—you don't want to dig around in there. It wouldn't be gold nuggets you'd be finding, if you know what I'm saying. Still, there wasn't much I could do. Razor Cannelloni was one of the last members of the Figanewty Mafia. He was one kid you didn't mess with.

"I just can't watch them dig anymore." A single feather dislodged from somewhere behind Pigeon's ear and fluttered to the ground. I know what you're thinking . . . feathers? But you have to understand Pigeon didn't earn his nickname just because he fluttered around the school, carrying messages to people. No, it was so much more than that. "They've filled an entire bag with what they're calling squishy gold nuggets! It's humiliating."

"Pigeon, have you tried telling them Razor was lying?" Snow Cone asked.

Pigeon blinked. "Can I do that, sir?" he whispered.

"Yes."

"Oh, thank you!" And with that, Pigeon vanished with a puff of feathers.

I sighed and massaged my thumb, warming it up for the tournament. We were always putting out fires on the playground. You can't thwart an evil plan to take over the school with a mind-controlling potion and not expect a wave of popularity to follow.

As we approached the marble arena, I saw some familiar faces. Radar Munsky, Joe Joe Pounder, and Giddy McElroy already had their marbles in the polisher, but there were two faces I didn't recognize. "Who's that?" I whispered to Snow.

Standing next to Radar, strawberry blonde hair flowing in the air like a sock puppet, was a new girl. She was tall, which was no surprise, since all the girls at Pordunce Elementary stared down upon the rest of us midgets, and she was pretty.

"I dunno," Snow Cone answered. "Maybe she's from another school."

I knew it. Eventually my reputation was bound to spread. I just didn't expect it to be so early in the year. There were always kids hanging around the arena, but this was the first time I had a fan from another school. Plus, she was a girl. I cracked my knuckles and gave the new girl a wink. She gave me the stink eye. They always play hard to get.

"Hashbrown, have you met Melanie 'Thumbs' Nottingham yet?" Radar asked, pointing to the new girl.

I smiled. "No, I haven't. Is she here to watch me take another trophy?"

Melanie flicked a lock of hair behind her ear. "Hardly," she said with a laugh.

"And that's her little brother, Nugget." Radar gestured toward a short, heavy-set boy, with an unusually round and freckled face. He was mashing his fingers violently on a handheld video game console. "They moved here yesterday. Melanie was the marbles champion at her old school."

"Really?" I asked, trying hard not to burst out laughing. Obviously, Melanie had told Radar that to impress him and now she was trying to impress me. A pesky fly buzzed around my head, and I swatted at it with the back of my hand. "So why do they call you Thumbs?"

It all happened so fast, I barely had time to react. One second the fly was hovering back and forth, loving life, and the next second something whizzed by my ear and the fly was splattered on the back of a shiny marble with an image of a skull embedded in the glass. The marble flew on, making a high-pitched whistle as it bounced off a tree and returned to Melanie's hand. I didn't even see her fire it.

"Whoa!" Radar shouted.

"Holy Mona Lisa!" Snow Cone added, equally impressed.

I instinctively ducked and grabbed my ear. It was warm, and I was pretty sure a patch of hair was missing on the side of my head where Melanie's marble had passed. The whistling sound still lingered in the air.

It seemed as though the whole playground had fallen silent and was looking in our direction. In my long history of playing marbles, I had never seen a shot quite like that.

"How did you do that?" Snow Cone asked.

Melanie shrugged as she wiped the gooey remains of the fly off her marble.

Where did she get that marble? I owned all the catalogs, and they knew me on a first-name basis at Merrill's Marble Emporium. I think I would've remembered a bull basher like that.

"It was a lucky shot," I said, rising to my feet. Melanie's eyes narrowed, and I felt my stomach churn. I turned toward the arena and almost plowed over Pigeon, who was standing behind me looking confused.

"Pigeon, aren't you supposed to be stopping the excavation at the Clump Box?" I asked.

"Well, I was, sir. But then I heard you whistle for me. What can I do for you?"

"That wasn't *him* whistling, Pigeon," Radar said with a smirk.

I felt my face flush red.

Everyone crowded around the marble arena as I stepped up for the final match. The first few games had been a breeze, but my semi-final match against Snow Cone turned out to be a real doozy. I ended up winning four games to one in our best of seven match-up, but I was proud of Snow. Last year, he didn't have a clue how to hold a marble, and now he was making it to the semi-finals.

Melanie Thumbs destroyed Radar in their semi-final match. It started off all right with Radar's first shot scattering four steelies. But Melanie never gave him another chance to shoot. In a blinding blur, she wiped the arena clean in what became the fastest elimination in the history of Pordunce.

Now Melanie and I faced off across the center ring. Still standing behind her, smacking his video game like it was a disobedient goat, was Nugget.

"Aha!" Nugget cheered, pumping his fist. "Thirty thousand points!" He flashed the screen of the video game toward the crowd. At first no one said anything. Then Nugget's eyes began to bulge, and we all cheered along with him, trying to sound as excited as we could. Echo Rodriguez patted him on the shoulder, and Nugget's whole head began to shake.

"Geez, take it easy, buddy," Echo said. "Take it easy, buddy," he repeated.

I won the coin toss and decided to take the first shot. I'd be lying if I said I wasn't a little worried because this girl could definitely play.

I stared at the circle of marbles, swung my head to the side, and fired my bull basher, scattering seven steelies and two shooters out of the center ring. It was a glorious shot, and the crowd erupted with cheers. I smiled apologetically at Melanie. Because I'd knocked two of her shooters out of the circle, I could choose to take another shot and go for the win by knocking out her last shooter. If I hit it, the game was over. If I missed, she would win. It was a bonus shot, and it was risky. But something told me if I took the easy way out, Melanie would not give me another chance.

I plucked my bull basher from the center ring and rubbed it against my shirt. "I think I'll go for the win." This caused an immediate outburst of cheers.

"What do you mean go for the win?" Radar asked from the crowd. "Did I hear you right?" And of course he had. Radar's ears had been known to pick up conversations on jumbo jets, flying miles above the school.

"What's going on?" Four Hips Dixon asked as he circled around the outside of the crowd, selling concessions. It was his regular job during all marble tournaments, but he had yet to sell a single snack. Most people didn't like having to wrestle for a corn dog, and Four Hips never gave up easily.

"Hashbrown's taking a bonus shot!" Joe Joe Pounder said above the steadily growing uproar.

I owned this playground. Tucking my thumb behind my bull basher, I raised one hand to silence the crowd. I stared over at Melanie, and she was fuming. It was awesome!

I caught sight of several of my other friends pushing their way to the front. Whiz Peterson, Measles Mumphrey, and Bubblegum Bulkins had come to see the final match.

"What's up guys? Ready to see history?" I asked. Whiz and Measles stared at the ground, not wanting to make eye contact with me. Maybe they didn't want to jinx my luck. Bubblegum had probably swallowed too much gum during lunch because he looked sick.

"Hey, I have to tell you something," Bubblegum said in a depressing voice.

"It'll have to wait until after I take this trophy," I said. Couldn't he see I was involved in something important? I honed in on the target and readied my thumb for the attack.

"Hashbrown, my dad got a new job."

"Good for him," I said, sighing. "Now, will you please be quiet?"

"We're moving."

My marble fired wide, missing the circle completely and soaring across the playground to where it came to rest in the sandbox.

"Eureka! We've found the mother lode!" I faintly heard Prospector Pete—a first-grader who wore a headlamp and carried a pick-axe to school every day—cry as he discovered my bull basher in between cat clumps and sand.

I had lost the match to Melanie Thumbs and had probably lost my bull basher as well, but that didn't matter. Swiveling around, I faced Bubblegum, who looked like he was on the verge of throwing up. In a matter of seconds, I'd fallen from the mountain top into the toilet.

Chapter **3**

The Manatee's Friendly Advice

I couldn't sleep that night. I hadn't lost a marble match in over two years. Oh, how I despised that Melanie—with her smug little grin and her long flowing hair.

Then there was Bubblegum, moving away forever in two weeks. How could this be happening? This type of stuff wasn't supposed to happen in elementary school. Who was going to entertain me now in Mr. Blindside's social studies class? Bubblegum could blow the best balloon animals, and they always smelled of whatever he'd eaten for breakfast. It just wasn't fair. Bubblegum's dad had been a gourmet chef at Tootie's Mexican Restaurant since before we were born. Why did he have to take another job?

The next morning I stumbled to my locker. Exhausted and depressed, I cycled through my combination.

"How did you sleep?" Snow Cone asked, leaning up against the locker next to mine.

"How do you think?" I replied.

"I figured. Look, I've come to warn you about Hambone." Snow Cone leaned in close.

"What about him?" I asked.

"Something's got him spooked. He's lashing out at

everyone he comes in contact with."

"What do you mean 'spooked'?" I looked down the hall to my left just as Hambone appeared, dragging Fibber Mckenzie behind him by his collar.

"This is your last chance," Hambone growled. "Was it you?"

Fibber squirmed, trying to break free from Hambone's clutches.

"I told you, it wasn't me!" Fibber pleaded. "I don't even go to this school. I just work here."

Poor Fibber, whether or not he was guilty, he was not the best person to defend himself. He had no control over the lies that came out of his mouth.

"That's it!" Hambone wrenched open the nearest locker. Flinging Fibber through the opening, he slammed the door shut and glared at everyone. "No one goes near this locker until I get to the bottom of this!" Turning so hard on his heels that some of the floor tiles cracked beneath his weight, Hambone stormed off.

Silence engulfed the fifth-grade wing.

"What's gotten into him?" I whispered.

"Word on the street is, Hambone saw something in one of the classrooms. Something that shouldn't have been there."

"Like what?"

"I don't know, but I do know the reason Principal Herringtoe extended recess yesterday wasn't because of ter-mites. Most of the teachers are spooked as well. And to make matters worse, I've heard the Oracle's in a really bad mood."

"The Oracle's always in a bad mood," I said. Gabriel "The Oracle" Yucatan had been trapped in his locker for over seven years. It was bound to make you a little irritated.

"Not like this," Snow Cone continued. "Apparently, some confused second-grader crammed all sorts of junk in the Oracle's locker slot the other day. You know how easily second-graders get lost at Pordunce."

I nodded. It was common knowledge that something happened to a kid once he graduated first grade and entered second. It's hard to explain, but kids get sucked into some sort of mind vortex. Kindergarteners and first graders get to eat paste and sing "Happy Letter" songs. Second grade is when homework really starts and teachers hand out detentions. That sort of stress takes its toll. It's common to see second graders trying to sit down at the fifth-grade lunch table or popping out of Mr. Buse's trash can wearing a pizza delivery jacket. Sad, really.

"What sort of junk?" I asked.

"Oh you know, yo-yos, bubblegum wrappers, I think a dog whistle too. The usual second-grade junk, but I'm telling you, something's amiss at Pordunce." Snow Cone looked in either direction. "I'd watch your back if I were you."

Melanie Thumbs rounded the corner, holding the prestigious marble trophy in her arms and beaming from ear to ear. My hand closed around a piece of paper in my locker, crumpling it into a wad. Snow Cone grabbed my wrist.

"Don't," he warned. Nugget was right behind her, still engrossed in his video game. "He may only be in kindergarten, but I hear he bites with the best of them."

I eased my grip off the wad of paper. "I don't like her. These are our glory years, Snow, and she's gonna ruin them."

"Don't worry. You'll get your chance at redemption."

I grabbed the edge of my locker and just about slammed it shut on Snow Cone's hand.

"Whoa, hold up!" he said, pushing my locker back open. He reached in, grabbed a small note taped to the back of my locker, and opened it. Together we read the strange message.

Hashbrown, it's time I call in my favor. Come quickly and come alone.

—Twinkles

"Uh-oh," I whispered.

Snow Cone's eyes whirled. "Twinkles? Isn't he the guy that gave you the stink bomb? What does he mean by calling in a favor?"

Marlow "Twinkles" Tanner was responsible for landing me in more trouble than I can remember. He lived beneath the school and sold junk out of his pawn shop to anyone who stumbled upon his store. One of the last things he said to me before selling me the world's worst stink bomb, disguised as a time machine, was that one day I'd have to return the favor.

"How did he get into your locker?" Snow Cone asked.

"My uncle has his ways," a voice bellowed.

All right, I'll admit it, I squealed, but you would've done the same thing if you'd turned around and come face-to-face with Luinda's abnormally large head.

You may or may not already know Luinda Sharpie. If you subscribe to *Texas Turnbuckle Magazine*, then the name will sound familiar. Yep, she's the same Luinda Sharpie, also known as "The Manatee," who won the heavyweight belt from Ronick the Romping Russian at last month's amateur wrestling invitational. Oh, and she's also Hambone Oxcart's girlfriend. You don't want to get on her bad side.

"Good grief! Don't sneak up on us like that!" I said, pressing my back up against the locker and clutching at my chest in search of a heartbeat.

Luinda giggled. "Sorry, but I was told to make sure you got that message. It's pretty important."

Twinkles was Luinda's favorite uncle. It was strange to think of her having any family. I just assumed she lived at some wrestling gym and slept every night in the ring.

"Uh . . . Luinda," I said, trying to inch my way around her. "I don't have time to go see Twinkles right now."

Luinda popped the thumb knuckle on her right hand, sounding like she was cocking a shotgun. To be honest, there isn't really much of a difference. "Oh, you don't, huh?"

Mr. Coppercork appeared from his classroom and scampered toward us, ruler in hand.

"The bell's already rung for first period, Hashbrown, and if you're late one more time for class, I'll have no choice but to give you detention."

Detention? That wasn't an option. I had too many things to do after school to be wasting my time smacking erasers together for Mr. Coppercork.

"You're not off the hook, Hashbrown." Luinda tapped her toe against the floor. "My uncle needs to see you."

"But, Luinda," I said. "We've got a lot of things to do and we're really busy with all the . . . planning and the . . . um . . ." My eyes shifted over to Snow Cone.

"Yeah, right." Snow Cone's head bounced like a bobblehead doll. "Lots of homework, and tests, and . . ."

Luinda's hand slowly folded into a fist. "I see." A vein in the shape of a pitchfork bulged on her forehead. "I guess you don't have to go. I'm sure Uncle Twinkles will understand. Say, have I ever showed you my newest wrestling move?"

I shot a sideways glance at Snow Cone and our eyes met. I had no idea what sort of torture Luinda "The Manatee" Sharpie could put me through, but I wasn't eager to find out.

"You know, I suppose I owe Twinkles a quick visit. It's the least I could do."

Luinda smiled, but I detected a hint of sadness on her face, as if she'd been looking forward to introducing my nose to the back of my heels.

Chapter 4

Hamsters and Stink Bombs

Twenty minutes later, my mind still raced with the events of the morning. Hambone always crammed people into lockers, but this was different. I had heard only a few things could frighten him, and they weren't your normal things like jelly doughnuts, drive-thru window menus, and the talking poster of a giant pineapple at Marty Muffits Grocery store. To see Hambone worried was disturbing.

And now I had to visit Twinkles's Pawn Shop.

Suddenly, thunder boomed overhead, and the lights went out. Someone screamed, and I covered my ears, looking around. Cup o' Noodle Hickok had flung his head back and was screaming so loudly, the windows started to rattle. Apparently, he'd tried to sneak a sip of broccoli cheese soup from his pants pocket during the lesson, and when the power went out, he'd accidentally rammed the straw up his nose.

Mr. Coppercork tried to calm him down, but Cup o' Noodle reared back and sneezed, sending a spray of orange soup and other nose debris all over the classroom. It was utter mayhem, and I couldn't think of a more perfect opportunity to sneak out of class and down to Twinkles's pawn shop. Luckily, there were so many people dodging his cheesy boogers that it created just enough distraction for me to slip out of the room unnoticed.

The hallways were empty as I tiptoed toward the fourth-grade wing. Peering over both shoulders to ensure the coast was clear, I pressed my hand against what looked like just some ordinary wall but was in fact a hidden passageway. Pulling back the curtain, I stared down into the darkness of the Secret Stairwell.

Twinkles's pawn shop looked exactly how it had the last time I'd visited. Piles of dirty laundry and fish stick boxes hedged up the way. Junk teetered everywhere in towering stacks. Dogs and cats perched on every countertop, watching me tiptoe around a table brimming with cans of soup. I had to watch where I stepped as little plastic balls, filled with dizzy hamsters, raced under my feet. It was like I was the only one who had a ticket to the world's weirdest circus, and I wanted my money back.

Twinkles sat slumped in a rocking chair in the corner of the room, his face buried in his hands. He was old and skinny with a few wisps of gray hair dancing in the breeze of a circulating fan.

"You wanted to see me?" I nearly tripped over a rogue hamster ball.

Twinkles's head shot up, and his eyes blazed with excitement. "I'm so glad you came!" he shouted. "Things have been bad here, lately. Lots of problems."

My foot nudged something soft and squishy on the floor. It could've been a giant marshmallow, but I'm pretty sure I heard it cough right before it slithered under the table. "Problems?" I asked, deciding the safest spot in the shop was standing on a stool next to Twinkles's chair.

"It's just so awful," he muttered, his forehead plopping back into his hands.

"What happened?" I asked.

"Pepper and Siegfried are gone!" His shoulders trembled.

"Ah, I see," I said. I didn't have a clue what he was talking about. "Who are Siegfried and Pepper?"

"My hamsters, of course."

Of course, I thought, looking around at half a dozen other hamsters chattering at each other. "What exactly are these things, then?"

Twinkles looked up, his eyes raw and puffy. "Those are hamsters too. But Siegfried and Pepper were my favorite pets. That's why I asked you to come. I need a favor."

What was I supposed to do? "Uh, I'm sorry to hear about your hamsters. It must be hard when your pets run away, but—"

"They didn't run away! Something wicked took them." His eyes widened.

"What do you mean, 'something wicked'?" I asked.

Twinkles wiped his nose with the back of his hand. "Best if I show you." He snatched hold of my arm and hopped up from the rocking chair.

I was pretty sure I didn't need to see for myself. In fact, I had no desire to follow Twinkles out into the dark. Besides, I had to get back to class before things finally settled and Mr. Coppercork realized I was missing.

"This way, Hashbrown, just a little farther," Twinkles muttered as he dragged me along behind him. We approached a gaping hole in the wall at the end of the path. Rock crumbled down from a large crack that opened into a deep ravine. Twinkles pointed into the darkness.

"A couple nights ago, my hamsters crashed into this wall and woke something up. I've never seen anything like it."

"What was it?"

"A ghost, Hashbrown!" Twinkles's voice rose with

excitement. "It's evil, and it took my hamsters."

I used to believe in ghosts until I discovered the haunted house down at the end of my road was really owned by a man with irritable bowel syndrome. "Why would a ghost take your hamsters?"

"I don't know, but I'm scared for Siegfried and Pepper. They've never been away this long before. Who's going to feed them their vitamins?"

I kicked a rock with my shoe and sent it skipping through the hole. A hollow echoing sound filled the quiet passage as the rock traveled far out of sight. "What do you want me to do?"

"Bring them back."

I flinched. "Bring them back? But didn't you say a ghost took them?"

He nodded.

"How am I supposed to bring back your hamsters if a ghost has them?" The old man had lost it. "I'm sorry, but I can't help you."

Twinkles eyes flashed with anger. "But you said you'd return the favor. How can you tell me no after all I've done for you?"

I laughed. "I asked you for a time machine and you gave me the world's worst stink bomb. I almost got kicked out of school!"

"Things turned out all right, didn't they? You saved the day and got your friends back. Isn't that what you wanted? You probably just pushed the wrong button."

"There was only one button, and it didn't open up a portal to another time. It unleashed a tornado of poo!"

Twinkles glanced back down the passage toward his shop. "I have more of them in my shop, you know."

"More what? Stink bombs? Why would I want another

one of those?" Truthfully, I would've loved to own at least a dozen more of those stink bombs. They could solve so many of my problems.

Twinkles's eyes sparkled sinisterly. "Oh, I wouldn't just give you a stink bomb. Clearly, you don't see their value. But what I could do is plant a few of those bombs where you wouldn't want them. I'd hate to think of what could happen to your precious little tree house if six stink bombs exploded during your next club meeting. That could get a tad . . . nasty, if you know what I mean."

Oh, boy. *Now* I understood where he was going with this. Those bombs, in the wrong hands, were deadly. Just one of them could destroy my tree house, drenching it in a stench that could never be removed. Six of them? Well, that would be the end of the neighborhood.

"You wouldn't dare do that," I said, backing away until my shoulder blades pressed against the far wall.

"I'm sorry, but you've left me with no other choice." He pulled a remote control and a photograph from his pocket. "I figured you'd be difficult." He passed me the photograph and I gasped, recognizing the image of my tree house. Wired at the base of the tree, on the ladder and on each of the corner posts, were six silver orbs—stink bombs rigged to explode.

"I control them with this." He waved the controller in his hand. "And don't even think of trying to defuse the bombs. I'll be watching."

"But we can still work this out," I pleaded.

"I'm afraid not. I have to do this to save my pets. You have three days to find the ghost and bring them back." Twinkles spun on his feet, his heels clacking, and stormed off down the passage.

Chapter 5

Down the Splashing Barrel

Snow Cone was in the halls when I stumbled to my locker. This was terrible. Why did I have to be the one to solve the mystery of Twinkles's missing hamsters? I had too many things on my plate to be worrying about his problems.

"Strange day, huh?" Snow Cone asked as more thunder rumbled overhead.

"No kidding. Groundhog may have predicted an early spring, but this is ridiculous."

Snow Cone nodded. "Hey, I've got some good news."

"I could use some good news right about now."

"Ms. Borfish called in sick yet again." Snow Cone beamed.

"Two days in a row?" I asked. "That's never happened before." I should've been excited. Every kid dreaded lunch because Ms. Borfish ran the cafeteria at Pordunce Elementary. But instead of jumping for joy, my shoulders managed a slight shrug.

"What's gotten into you?"

I ran my fingers through my hair. *"The hundred-acre woods are full of boll weevils,"* I whispered.

Snow Cone raised an eyebrow and started to laugh. "No

she isn't. Don't be ridiculous. You're mom's too skinny to be a sumo wrestler." He laughed even harder and playfully slugged me in the shoulder.

I smacked my forehead. "Not bull weasels, Snow, *boll weevils.*"

Snow Cone's laughter tapered into a soft chuckle. His eyes darted back and forth as he successfully translated the code. "Six stink bombs? Why would he do that?" Snow Cone covered his mouth with his hands. "It'll destroy the tree house!"

"I know!" I snapped.

"Well, what does he want you to do?"

I took a deep breath and told him everything that had happened down in Twinkles's pawn shop.

Snow Cone pulled out his clipboard and jotted a few notes on one of the pages. "So, do you really think there's a ghost?" he asked.

Before I could answer, Whiz rounded the corner, a look of panic etched on his face and a stream of yellow trailing in his wake. He didn't seem to notice where he was running, and before we could get out of the way, he collided with the two of us.

Whiz let out a blood-curdling scream. "Please don't eat me! Please don't eat me!" he begged, his whole body shaking.

"Whiz!" I shouted. "What's going on?"

He snapped out of his terror and looked up at me in shock. "Hashbrown, is that really you?"

"Of course it's me. Who did you expect?"

Whiz peered back over his shoulder. "Something . . ." he squeaked. "Something was down there."

"Down where?" Snow Cone asked, causing Whiz to squeal again.

"Sorry, Snow. I didn't see you there," Whiz apologized.

"You're lying in my lap, how could you not . . . ? Oh, Whiz! These are my favorite jeans!" Snow Cone pushed Whiz off his lap and fumed.

"What's with the barrel?" I looked down at Whiz's strange choice in clothing.

"My mom always makes me wear a barrel whenever there's a thunderstorm."

"Well, it's not doing its job now, is it?" Snow Cone said.

"Never mind that, Snow." I helped Whiz to his feet. "What were you running from?"

"I don't know what it was, but it wasn't natural." Whiz pointed toward the hallway connecting the fourth- and fifth-grade wings, and Snow Cone and I followed his finger. There was nothing there. The hall was empty.

"I swear it was there just a second ago," Whiz whispered. "It tried to grab me!"

"What tried to grab you?" I demanded. "What did it look like?" Was this the lead we needed to find Twinkles hamsters? Sweat beaded up on my forehead.

"It was all white and very tall," Whiz whispered, his voice shaking with panic. "I think . . . I think it was a . . ."

The lights in the hallway flickered and went out as thunder clapped outside.

"The power's out again!" I shouted. I looked at Snow Cone, but he had fallen silent, his eyes wide and fearful. I spun around and gasped as the doorknob of an unused classroom at the end of the hallway began to jiggle. Something was trying to come out. Whiz whimpered and tried to hug me, but I pushed him away with my foot.

A red light poured out from beneath the door. I wanted to scream and run back to my classroom, but I couldn't move.

Was Pordunce actually haunted?

Just then, the lights overhead hummed and flashed back into life. The red glow disappeared, and the jiggling door-knob ceased. The three of us breathed heavily.

"Okay, what in the world was—?" Snow Cone stopped mid-sentence as the door at the end of the hallway opened and Melanie Thumbs walked out. I was so surprised to see her emerging from the abandoned classroom, I nearly joined Whiz in his barrel. Nearly, mind you.

Melanie jumped back in alarm when she saw us gawk-ing at her. "What are you doofuses staring at?" she shouted, resting her hands on her hips.

At first, the three of us were speechless, but as the horror wore off, I regained my ability to talk. "Maybe we should be asking you the same question."

"Are you calling me a doofus?"

Snow Cone and Whiz immediately shook their heads, but I nodded. "Well, if the shoe fits."

Melanie's hand shot for her pocket and pulled out the familiar bull basher with a skull. "I think you'd better watch what you say, Hashbrown, or I'll buzz your other ear."

"Oh yeah, why don't you explain what you were doing in that room?" I asked, cupping my hands over my ears for protection.

"That's none of your business." Melanie kept her marble aimed at my head.

Aha! The little prankster was up to something, and we had caught her red-handed.

"You better believe it's our business," I shouted back. Melanie's hand seemed to be on the verge of firing. If she could hit a moving fly from two yards away, she could defi-nitely hit something of value on my face from this distance. "I think you owe us an explanation."

"I don't owe you anything," Melanie said.

"Oh yeah, well something tells me you're the one running around scaring everybody."

Melanie started to grin. "What are you talking about?"

"First it was Hambone, and then it was Whiz. And I bet you've been down beneath the school as well. Haven't you? Stealing hamsters now, are we?"

She twirled her finger in the air by her ear. "Are you crazy? There's nothing beneath this school. And why would I steal hamsters?"

"No one uses that classroom anymore, so you have no reason to go in there, and we saw that red light. You've got some explaining to do."

"You're ridiculous." Melanie sighed. "But if you must know, I was putting my new trophy in a safe place. Mr. Buse is cleaning the trophy case today, and I didn't want to leave my prize out where someone could break it. He told me I could store it in here until he's done cleaning."

I looked at Snow Cone, who pulled out his clipboard. After thumbing through a few pages, his shoulders sagged a little, and he leaned in close to my ear.

"She's right about the trophy case," he whispered. "Mr. Buse scheduled a cleaning three weeks ago."

I leaned over Snow's shoulder to verify the date and grunted in agreement. "Maybe she's not lying about that," I whispered to Snow, "but she's hiding something else, and I'd bet its Siegfried and Pepper." I raised my voice and pointed a finger in Melanie's direction. "I'm not convinced!"

Melanie lowered her weapon. "Fine. Don't believe me? Have a look for yourself." She opened the door wider and gave the three of us a clear view of the trophy resting on one of the desks. I walked the length of the hallway with Snow Cone following close behind. Whiz, still too terrified to move, opted to retreat entirely into his barrel. The soft playful sounds of splashing rose up from beneath the lid.

I scanned the room in search of Twinkles's hamsters, but other than the trophy, the classroom was empty.

"Okay," Snow Cone said. "What about that red light. We all saw it coming from the room. How do you explain that?"

Melanie rolled her eyes. "You boys and your imaginations."

"Aha! Forty thousand points!"

Snow Cone and I jumped into each other's arms as Nugget's hand shot out from beside the door, flashing the screen of his video game for us to see. A bright red light blipped his high score. "Read it and weep!" he said, joining Melanie in the doorway. "That has to be a school record." Nugget shook his video game under my nose, and I felt the sudden urge to swat at it like it was a praying mantis. That little kindergartner was getting on my nerves.

Melanie huffed and Nugget stuck out his tongue as the two brushed past.

As we watched them disappear around the corner, I said, "I don't buy it. She's up to something, and her little brother has to be in on it."

"Maybe," Snow Cone agreed. "Or maybe we just freaked out for no reason."

I nodded, but my mind was still swirling. How was I going to solve this mystery? My tree house was in danger, and I had no idea where I was going to find those hamsters. Something tapped me sharply on my shoulder, and I spun around to face Mr. Coppercork and his wooden ruler.

"Looks like you'll be spending this afternoon with me and my erasers after all," he said with a grin.

Chapter 6

Hashbrown's Squawking Walkie

Later that evening, after a long afternoon of beating erasers with a wooden mallet, I sat on my bed and stared at a picture resting on my dresser. It was an image of me, Bubblegum, Snow Cone, and Measles riding the log flume at Mohari Mongoose's Amusement Park last summer. Our hands were in the air as water splashed all around us. Whiz and Four Hips had been at the park too but were unable to join us on the log flume for obvious reasons. Every water park in the tri-state area has a mug shot of Whiz Peterson drinking a Big Slurp. And Four Hips had to ride alone unless Pigeon was wearing high heels in order to make him taller than Mohari's armpit on the "You Must Be This Tall to Ride" sign.

My club had grown so much since that fun-filled day at Mohari's. Now, we had a total of eleven members. We held monthly seminars and workshops, and just last week, I received a letter from a fifth-grader in an elementary school three hours away, asking me if I'd ever considered starting a franchise of tree houses. There were dozens of kids willing to do whatever it took to be in my club, but none of them could ever replace Bubblegum. He was an original member, and in two weeks he would be gone. My throat tightened as I walked to my window and stared out at my tree house.

Even in the darkness, I could see the shadowed outlines of the stink bombs strapped to the beams.

The emergency walkie-talkie on my desk chirped, causing me to suck back on my teeth. It'd been nearly three months since an incident had escalated to the point where we needed to communicate on the emergency walkie-talkies, and that one had involved Principal Herringtoe, his pet emu, and a twenty-gallon tub of dill dip. I dove across the room, snatching up the walkie-talkie.

"Code in," I ordered, holding the transmitter button.

There was a pause, and then static crackled as a familiar voice rose from the receiver. *"The flea circus leaves in the morning, and I'm feeling itchy."*

I breathed a sigh of relief. "Go ahead, Snow Cone. What's going on?"

"We have an emergency, Hashbrown. You better come to Pordunce quickly," Snow's voice said in a serious tone. "It's Bubblegum . . . something terrible has happened."

I gripped the walkie-talkie with both hands. "What happened to him?" Had his family decided two weeks was too long to wait? Were they moving tonight?

Snow Cone fell silent on the other end. I waited as static filled the eerie, night air. Finally he said, *"Sometimes I dream that he is me. Like Mike, I want to be like Mike!"*

I stared at the walkie as the static ceased and Snow's voice vanished completely. Maybe Snow Cone had made a mistake. I reached under my desk and ripped my copy of our secret code language reference from its velcro strap. There was no need to search; I knew every code in this book. But for some reason, I had to make sure. I scanned through until I found the page containing Snow Cone's secret message, confirming what I already knew: Bubblegum was trapped inside Pordunce Elementary, and to make matters worse, he wasn't alone.

Chapter 7

New Recruits?

"Hummus, this stuff's disgusting!" Measles complained, spitting out a gob of brownish goop onto the ground of the parking lot just outside of Pordunce.

"Oh, but it's so good for you," Hummus Laredo said. He raised the plastic jar to his nose and breathed in the aroma. "Worm paste is one of the healthiest alternatives to beef."

At the mention of worm paste, everyone in the group gagged and spat out whatever was in their mouths.

"Worm paste?" Snow Cone wiped the slime from his lips. "Why didn't you tell us what it was before we ate it?"

Everyone was grossed out—everyone except for Pigeon, who continued to sneak his fingers into Hummus's jar and stole off in the shadows to enjoy his snack. I had learned not to eat anything out of Hummus's strange jars. My focus was trained on the school building looming in the shadows ahead. Bubblegum was hiding in there somewhere, and it was up to us to get him out.

"Are you guys through eating?" I asked, unable to hide my annoyance. My friends had all come quickly once Snow Cone had set off the alarm, but their nerves were shaken. This was not just some practice drill. This was for real.

Snow Cone finished wiping his mouth on his sleeve and held out a gray homing device, pointing to a dull green blip that showed Bubblegum's location. The blip flashed with a soft squeaking sound.

"Right, give me the rundown." I was all business.

"At exactly 8:30 PM, I received the distress signal from Bubblegum on his emergency transmitter." Snow Cone held up the transmitter and a series of sharp beeps and boops flowed out of the receiver. "It's Morse code, and unless Bubblegum has just been playing with the buttons, this message is crystal clear: he's been forced into hiding somewhere in the school."

"Forced?" Whiz asked. "Who's forcing him?" Whiz was completely decked out in authentic spy gear. He wore a camouflaged jacket, a pair of night-vision goggles on his forehead, and military-style combat boots. Had it not been for his bright yellow pants, hand-sewn together by his mother out of rain slicker material, none of us would've recognized him.

Snow Cone replayed the ending of the coded message. "Unless I'm mistaken, there's some sort of phantom in there with him."

A hushed silence broke through the crowd. Pigeon fainted, crumpling into a heap on the ground. The poor little guy wasn't used to dealing with spirits. I scooted him off to the side of the parking lot and covered his tiny body with a blanket. He cooed peacefully in his sleep and continued to smack his lips around a gob of worm paste.

"A ghost in Pordunce!" Butter Bibowski said in disbelief as I rejoined the group. "How's this even possible?"

"It's not that hard to believe." Snow Cone tucked the transmitter in his back pocket. "We've all heard the rumors about the ancient burial grounds beneath the septic tank."

"But those are just rumors," Whiz said.

"There are never just rumors at Pordunce," I reminded him. "So, here's the game plan." I unrolled my own copy of Pordunce's blueprints and laid it out on the ground. "We get in, get Bubblegum, and get out as quickly as possible. Until we know what it is we're up against, we're not taking any chances—even to snag Twinkles's hamsters. I want this clean and professional. You got me?" Everyone nodded. "We'll break up into two teams. Snow Cone, you take Whiz, Butter, Mensa, Gavin, and Yeti and head through the entrances located here at the rear of the school." I circled the doors with a pencil. "Hummus, Measles, and Four Hips will follow me through the front. Is everyone ready?" I rolled up the blueprints and stuffed them in my backpack.

"Sure, but who are we going with?" someone asked.

The voice caught me off guard. I looked through the row of my friends' faces and felt an icky pit form in my stomach. Standing between a bewildered Four Hips and Measles were Melanie Thumbs and Nugget Nottingham.

"Wha—huh?" I blurted. What were they doing here?

"Sorry to surprise you, but you guys really need to change the station you use for your so-called 'emergency' walkie-talkie. Anyone listening in would've known you were headed to the school." Melanie held up her own walkie-talkie and giggled. She was dressed in an all-black sweat suit with black high-top sneakers. A utility belt draped around her waist bulged with several snap pouches. Her hair was pulled tightly into a ponytail, held back with a black scrunchie. Nugget was also dressed in a black sweat suit, but his face was yet again plastered to one of his video games.

I looked at Snow Cone in disbelief. "You can't be here!" I said, my voice rising with agitation.

"Sure I can," she responded. "You don't own this school.

I can come here whenever I want." She rested an elbow on Nugget's shoulder, and the little kindergartner flashed a dangerous glare in my direction.

"Look, Thumbs, I know you and I have our problems, but now's not the time to start this."

"I don't have a problem with you." Melanie batted her long eyelashes. "Why would I have a problem with someone I destroyed in a marble tournament? Being mean to you would be like being mean to a small, lost puppy. That would just be cruel."

My lips quivered like the opening of a very large and noisy whoopee cushion, and I could feel the tops of my ears turning a piercing shade of red. Something awful was going to explode from my mouth—something that would make Melanie Thumbs run away screaming. But before I could unleash my disastrous words, she spoke first.

"Besides, it's not like there's really an emergency here."

"What do you mean not an emergency?" Whiz asked. "Our friend Bubblegum is trapped somewhere in there." Whiz pointed in the wrong direction, toward the highway, but we all understood what he meant.

"Oh, I heard everything Hashbrown just told you loud and clear," she said. "But I doubt there's a real ghost. Your friend probably just got frightened by his own shadow. Judging by how scared you all look right now, it's not hard to imagine."

What a horrible person! If she hadn't been a girl—and capable of pounding me into a flour tortilla—I would've cartwheel kicked that smug smile right off her glittery lips.

I needed to remain calm. Exploding into a fit of rage was not fitting behavior for the leader of an elite tree house club. I knew what she was doing. She was trying to make me lose my cool.

"If you're so positive there's nothing to worry about inside Pordunce, then why did you come here tonight?"

Melanie fidgeted. "I left my trophy here today. I wouldn't dream of leaving it unprotected while a bunch of morons go rampaging through the school."

Four Hips's eyes widened as he looked up from his half-eaten turkey leg. "What's she talking about? Who else is coming to the school tonight?"

"We're not here for your dumb trophy, Thumbs." I tossed Four Hips a bag of corn nuts to put my confused friend's stress at ease. "So you can go on back home and leave us to do our work."

"Oh no. I'm not falling for that. If you're going in there, so am I." Melanie put her hands on her hips defiantly.

"Fine." I turned on my heels. "It's okay, guys, we're here to save Bubblegum, and that's what we're going to do. But you stay out of our way." I pointed to Melanie and she smiled.

"You won't even know I'm there. Of course, you'll probably have your hands full with that ghost." Melanie nudged past me, headed toward the main entrances. Nugget wobbled past as well but not before extending his hand to show me his progress on his video game.

"Found a secret level. Bet you've never done that," he mumbled with pride.

As the two of them neared the front of the school, Snow Cone patted my shoulder. "Something tells me we're in for a dangerous night," he said, lowering his night vision goggles over his eyes.

"You got that right, Snow," I whispered. "A dangerous night, indeed."

Chapter 8

The Mysterious Melanie Thumbs

There aren't too many students who know how to get into the school after Mr. Hackerfits, the janitor, locks up for the night. Every obstacle imaginable is attached to those doors. There are dead bolts, fake door knobs, razor wire, and one of the most expensive laser alarm systems in the county. Why the school's so heavily guarded, I really don't know, but it probably has to do with Principal Herringtoe's costume collection.

Whatever the case, there really aren't too many students that know how to get in, but *I* am one of them. Peering over my shoulder, making sure Melanie wasn't watching, I pressed my foot on top of a rotten tree stump and a hidden door opened up just behind the bike racks. I took a few minutes to weasel my way through the opening and up to the other side of the entrance doors to dismantle the alarm system.

Pordunce Elementary was filled with these types of secrets, and I knew most of their locations.

"We're in," I spoke into my walkie-talkie.

"So are we," Snow Cone answered. "We'll head toward the front and meet you at your locker in fifteen minutes."

Over the next five minutes, we quietly made our way

through the dark hallways, scanning every nook and cranny for Bubblegum. The homing device didn't give specific locations. It just showed Bulkins was somewhere in the school. Melanie and Nugget broke off once we hit the fifth-grade wing and headed for the room where she'd stashed her trophy.

The walkie-talkie crackled. "Hashbrown, do you read me? Over," Snow Cone spoke.

"I read you, Snow. Are you having any luck?"

"Not yet. How about you?"

"Nothing," I answered. I removed a canteen from my backpack and took a long swig. I needed energy and Molten Cola always did the trick. I passed the canteen around to everyone except Measles. It didn't offend him since no one in his right mind would eat or drink after him. Instead, he opened his own canteen and swallowed his medications.

"Hashbrown . . ." Snow Cone whispered. "Something's wrong."

"What is it? And why are you whispering?"

"We're hearing noises over here." He sounded worried.

"Noises? Is it Bubblegum?"

There was a pause before Snow Cone spoke again. "I don't think so . . . It's something else." The line fizzled.

Everyone in my group held his breath as we listened. Over the roar of the furnace, a banging sound cut through the air. It was sharp and loud, like someone was smacking the lockers.

"Hashbrown, I'm scared." Four Hips's eyes were wider than I'd ever seen them, and his lips were coated in powdered sugar. In the distance, the sharp thudding sounds continued for a few seconds and then fell completely quiet.

I pressed the transmitter button on my walkie-talkie. "Snow Cone, are you all right? What was that sound?"

There was no response, just the soft sizzle of static. What if the worst had happened and Snow was being forced to fend off the ghost with his walkie-talkie? What if we'd all walked right into a trap?

The walkie-talkie chirped, and a voice grumbled on the other end. It wasn't speaking clearly, and the words were distorted by the signal button.

Another chirp was followed by two beeps, and then Snow Cone's voice finally returned.

"All right, that's enough, Yeti, I think we've fixed it. Hashbrown, do you copy?"

"What's going on?" I demanded, relieved to hear he was still alive.

"Sorry about that," Snow Cone said. "I don't know what that banging noise was, but it spooked Whiz, and I accidentally slipped in his . . . uh . . . well . . . you know. I dropped the walkie and it broke into like six pieces. Luckily, Gavin knew how to fix it and used some of Yeti's leg hair to wire it up."

I wiped the sweat from my brow.

"We've found Bubblegum," Snow Cone said.

"You did?" I asked, clutching the walkie-talkie close to my mouth. "Where?"

"He was hiding inside the vending machines in the first-grade wing. Still not sure how he got in there, and it was a bugger to get him out."

This was good news. I wanted out of this creepy school. "All right. Can you make it back to my locker safely?"

"Yep. We'll meet you there."

Three minutes later, I stood at my locker with Hummus, Four Hips, and Measles, awaiting the safe arrival of the others.

The sound of footsteps arose from around the corner. I

turned, expecting to see Snow Cone, but was disappointed when Melanie appeared toting her trophy in her arms.

"Why are you still here?" I grumbled. "You've got your trophy now; you don't have to hang out with us anymore."

"Relax," she said through a faint smile. "I'm just going to stop by my locker for a second."

"Where's Nugget?" I asked. "I thought you never went anywhere without him."

"Oh, he likes to pace whenever he plays his games. I'm sure he'll show up in a minute or two." She surveyed the four of us and turned the trophy ever so slightly in her hands so the name plate was visible. *Melanie "Thumbs" Nottingham— Champion of Pordunce.* "Where's your friend? Did the ghost get him?" She didn't laugh, but I knew a thousand spit wads would never be able to dim the sarcastic twinkle in her eyes.

I ignored her and looked away. Who cared about her stupid trophy anyway? I had plenty of trophies at my house; some of them were twice as large as Melanie's. But it wasn't important. What was important was that Bubblegum was safe.

A chorus of screaming rose up from two hallways over. It was Snow Cone and the others, and judging by the sounds of their voices, they weren't skipping gleefully to us.

Without thinking, I charged off toward the shouting. The others were right behind me, including Melanie. I didn't have time to protest. She could do what she wanted. Maybe I'd get lucky and the ghost would attack her first.

As we neared the turn-off toward the hallway, an eerie red glow lit up the darkness. It was much stronger than the red light we had seen early that day from Nugget's video game screen. This was something else. I didn't have time to hesitate. I released a mighty war cry and bounded toward the hallway.

Suddenly Melanie surged ahead, rounding the corner before I was even at the end of the lockers. Just as I readied myself to make the turn, there was a flash of white light, followed by the horrible sound of moaning.

I came around the corner and saw the ghost with my own eyes. It was taller than Melanie, towering up almost to the top of the lockers, and it was covered head to toe in what looked like a white, flowing robe. I stumbled, nearly collapsing as Measles and the others plowed into my back.

Another flash of white light appeared from out of nowhere. The light was so strong I had to shield my eyes. I blinked back into focus, expecting the worst. But as the light faded away, I could see that the ghost was no longer in the hallway. Up ahead, a pile of moving arms and kicking legs squirmed. Snow Cone was on top, trying to sift through what looked like a giant human pretzel. The red light faded, its trail slipping away under the door of the Forbidden Bathroom. I arrived just as Melanie was helping Snow Cone to his feet. In her left hand I could see a solid white marble.

Bubblegum was the next out of the pile. His eyes were wild, darting this way and that. "It came from out of the cafeteria. That thing's out to get me, I tell you!"

I patted Bubblegum's back and handed him my canteen. He was dying of thirst and drained the last of my Molten Cola.

"We should've been ready for it," Snow Cone said, looking down at his shoes in shame. "It caught me off guard. I should've been paying better attention." I could see he was taking the brunt of the blame.

"You did the best you could," I said. Snow forced a smile but couldn't look me in the eyes.

"It wasn't really Snow Cone's fault." Gavin Glasses's head was the next to poke up from the pile. He examined the lenses of his glasses and wiped them with his shirtsleeve. "We were distracted."

"Distracted?" I asked.

"We would've been ready for the attack had *he* not shown up." Gavin pointed to the bottom of the pile where Nugget sat, growling. Melanie trotted over and helped her brother up.

"Yeah, he was all jumping around, showing us his silly score on his game. We couldn't step around him because he was in the way," Whiz said.

"It's not my fault," Nugget growled. "I had to tell someone about my score."

"Then the ghost was right on top of us and it was trying to eat us!" Yeti chimed in. "If Melanie hadn't thrown one of her magic beads, we would've been goners."

I nodded. "Yeah, you guys are lucky to be ali—wait a minute. Magic beads?" I looked at Melanie's hand where she was trying to hide her marble. A light bulb flicked on in the back of my brain—probably a 60-watter. "You mean magic *marbles*! Just what kind of marbles are those?"

"Uh . . . well . . . these are just . . ." Melanie stared at her marble and then at the floor. "They're just for emergencies."

"Sure, for emergencies and for winning marble tournaments! Let me see that," I demanded, reaching out to inspect one. Melanie quickly shifted out of the way.

"Are you suggesting I cheated in our match?" she asked, a dangerous glare in her eyes.

"That's exactly what I'm suggesting."

"Guys." Someone's voice spoke up from behind us, but we were too busy having a shouting match to listen.

"I never cheat!" Melanie's face came within inches of my nose. From this close, I could see her sparkly blue eyes very clearly. "I win fair and square."

"Whatever. You have magic, mystery marbles that blow up and flash lights and smash flies next to kids' ears. Why wouldn't you use one of those in a match?" This was my chance to prove I was still the best marble player at Pordunce.

"Oh, but you're forgetting something," she said, holding up a finger next to her face.

"Really, what's that?"

"Uh, guys, could you just take a breather for a second?" Again someone was trying to cut us off. Couldn't they see we were having a battle of words?

"I never got a chance to shoot." Melanie snapped her fingers. "You took a bonus shot and lost."

"A minor technicality. It doesn't change the fact that you probably cheated to beat Radar and you were going to cheat to beat me." Oh, I was on fire, using big words I really didn't know the meaning of and throwing facts in Melanie's face.

"GUYS!" Several of my friends shouted in unison, breaking my concentration.

"What is it?" I asked, spinning around in anger. Snow Cone, Whiz, and Four Hips were pointing their fingers at Nugget, who was starting to vibrate. His whole body shook as if he were standing right at the mouth of Krakatoa.

"What's wrong with your brother?" I asked.

"Is it an earthquake?" Four Hips clutched his cooler of food and shielded his head with a very large piece of Pita bread.

"It can't be an earthquake," Measles answered. "Today's not a Monday."

That made absolutely no sense whatsoever, but Measles was right about one thing—it wasn't an earthquake because we weren't shaking like Nugget.

"Nugget, what's going on?" Melanie asked with a calm and soothing voice.

Nugget's lips quivered. His cheeks puffed out, and his teeth chattered together. His eyes began to bulge like . . . well . . . like nuggets. Even the freckles dotting his face seemed to be growing bigger.

"Does he do this often?" I asked, taking a cautious step back from the troubled kindergartner.

"No, only when he's very angry about something."

"Is it because I piddled on him?" Whiz asked, moving behind me and out of Nugget's line of sight.

Nugget shook his head and held out his hands to show us the broken halves of his video game controller. During the scuffle with the ghost and the subsequent pile of kids, someone had crushed his most prized possession.

"This . . . this . . . is . . . not good . . ." Nugget rambled. "Someone . . . must . . . pay!" Nugget's eyes weren't even focused on anyone in particular.

"Easy, boy." I reached over to pat his arm.

"Don't touch him," Melanie warned.

I quickly pulled back my hand.

"Is he going to pop?" Butter asked from somewhere behind me.

"Nugget, it's nobody's fault," Melanie said. "No one was trying to crush your game. They were just scared because of the ghost." She pointed toward the bathroom door.

"I thought you didn't believe in ghosts," I said with an air of triumph.

"Do you think now's the best time to point that out?" Snow Cone stretched his head over my shoulder.

"Good call," I said, wondering why I was the one in front of everyone else.

Nugget's trembling head swiveled toward the bathroom door. "Oh . . . sweet . . . nuggets!" he shouted.

"Oh no!" Melanie screamed. "He's reached the point of no return!"

We were helpless to stop him. In a blinding fit of rage, Nugget charged toward the Forbidden Bathroom and burst through the door.

"Nugget, no! Don't go in there!" I shouted, but it was too late. We watched in shock and covered our noses as a cloud of gas escaped just before the door closed, sealing Nugget off from the free-breathing world.

"What's wrong with that bathroom?" Melanie asked, plugging up her nostrils with a couple of purple shooters. Where was she getting all of her marbles? She seemed to have an endless supply.

"That's the Forbidden Bathroom!" Whiz exclaimed. "You used to be able to go in there back in the olden days. It would just become a quarantined zone every day after second period because of Ms. Borfish. But ever since she started drying her own fruit, that restroom became off-limits for good. No one goes in the Forbidden Bathroom unprotected."

There was a loud thud, and something bumped the other side of the door. Melanie panicked, but as she rushed toward the bathroom to save her brother she was hit with a wall of stink. "Ugh! That's awful!" she shouted. "Nugget? Nugget, can you hear me?" There was no reply. Melanie spun around. "Someone has to help him," she demanded. "Please!" She looked straight at me, and I couldn't help myself.

I opened my backpack. "Don't anybody move!" I ordered, strapping on my gas mask. This was crazy. I didn't even like that kid. But I wouldn't wish the Forbidden Bathroom on my worst enemy. Everyone else backed far away from me as I struggled to open the door. Nugget had collapsed almost immediately when the cloud hit him, and his small, round body was forming a roadblock. The air swirled with poisonous stink. Even though I was wearing my gas mask, I wasn't about to linger any longer than necessary. I grabbed Nugget beneath his armpits and heaved him out of the danger zone, but not before scanning my perimeter for any signs of the ghost. Nothing else was in there. The spirit had disappeared.

Chapter 9

Schnukums and Sweet Cakes

There I sat, exhausted, in Miss Pinken's science class, holding my fourth beaker in my hand; the shattered remains of the other three were scattered around my desk. I was too nervous, and every time someone spoke too loudly, I would accidentally smash another beaker. Why did Vice Principal Humidor have to pick this day to announce parent-teacher conferences?

"Hashbrown." Someone called my name, and I broke the fourth beaker.

"Aha Kajah!" I screamed, diving beneath my chair. I looked up to see Miss Pinkens glaring down at me.

"For the last time, why are you breaking my beakers?" she asked.

"I'm sorry, but I'm a little jumpy right now. Maybe we should mix chemicals on another day."

"That's what I've been trying to tell you." Miss Pinkens tapped her foot sharply on the floor. "No one's mixing chemicals today. We're having an open book quiz on helium!"

I blinked and looked around the room at all of my classmates who were clutching their pencils and notebooks. They looked very worried. I was so confused. I needed to solve this mystery fast before I had a nervous breakdown.

Miss Pinkens must have realized the pressure I was feeling because she didn't immediately give me detention. Instead, she returned to the front of the classroom, and I sat back down in my chair as the bell sounded through the intercom, announcing class was over.

Outside a surprising number of students were crowded around Luinda Sharpie's store.

"What's going on?" I asked. "Are you having some sort of sale today?"

Luinda guffawed like a chimpanzee, the metal clasps of her braces glinting in the glow of the overhead lights. "I have no idea," she said. "Everyone's buying flashlights."

"Flashlights? Why flashlights?"

"It's because we heard the ghost doesn't like bright lights," said Squeaky Mittons, an unusually noisy third grader. He clicked on his own flashlight and unleashed a barrage of squeaks out of some unknown part of his body. "Melanie Thumbs scared off the ghost last night with some sort of light, and we're getting prepared."

I rubbed my eyes with my fingers, forcing myself to relax. "Let's get one thing straight," I said. "Melanie wasn't the only one fighting the ghost."

Several squeaks sounded as Squeaky Mittons hopped up and down in excitement. "Oh yeah, I almost forgot! Nugget was there too."

"Nugget?" I threw my hands up. "Are you kidding me? If it wasn't for me, Nugget would still be lying in the Forbidden Bathroom . . . suffocating."

This was just peachy. Just a couple of days ago Melanie had been a nobody. Now she was a marble champion and, according to Squeaky, Pordunce's very own ghost-slayer.

I sulked over to my locker and put in my combination.

"That's something you don't see every day." Snow Cone leaned up against the locker next to mine, watching the crowd gather around the store.

My heart pounded in my chest. "What am I going to do, Snow?" Just then an enormous shadow fell across my locker. Spinning around, I came face-to-face with a hairy belly button. Hambone must've accidentally shrunk his tank top because it wasn't covering much. One of Hambone's meaty mitts closed around my shirt collar, and I levitated off the floor until I was inches away from his stubbly chin.

"Was it you?" he growled. "Did you do it?"

My neck swiveled toward Snow Cone, desperately seeking his help, but my best friend was practicing his mannequin impersonation, and I must say he was in top form.

"Wha—what? Did I do what?" I stammered.

"Are you making that whistling sound?" Hambone pulled my head in closer, giving me a full-on view of his molars. "Phil can't stand it!"

As if beckoned by his name, an enormous cockroach scurried over the crest of Hambone's shoulder and peered down at me with quivering antennae. It was the first time I'd seen Hambone's pet cockroach in more than a month. Phil didn't like me much. You smash one insect with a bull basher, and they never forgive you.

"I'm not whistling," I insisted. My dangling arms and legs were falling asleep. "I don't even hear any whistling."

Hambone's nostrils flared. "It's too high for us to hear, but Phil hears it and he hates it. He says it hurts his ears." I nodded in agreement partly because I wanted to keep Hambone happy and partly because I myself had heard Phil talk before. "When I find out who it is whistling, I'm gonna—" Hambone's arms squeezed my shoulders so hard I felt air gush out of me like I was a broken bagpipe.

"Hambone, what are you doing to Hashbrown?" Luinda tapped him on the shoulder, and the squeezing eased. I gasped for air and blinked away hundreds of flashing blips that had formed in front of my eyes. Again I looked to Snow Cone for help, and again I found him striking a pose, standing as still as a statue. I couldn't blame him. The best thing you could do when Hambone was on the warpath was either be as helpful and agreeable as possible or, as in Snow Cone's case, fool Hambone with trickery.

"Uh, sweet cakes, I'm trying to stop that whistling." I almost laughed at the mention of Luinda's new nickname, but I quickly passed it off as a sneeze.

"Well, you don't really think it's Hashbrown, do you?" she asked.

"Urgh, no, I guess not." Hambone slowly lowered me until my feet touched the floor. "I don't like going to school here anymore. Seeing strange things in the classroom, power going out, and now that awful whistling. And it all started when I saw that weird groundhog!"

"Now, Hambone, you're not making any sense." Luinda patted his forearm.

"Yeah, it's not his fault this happened," I added, my words gasping out in between labored breaths. "Brummer didn't mean anything by it."

"Who?" Hambone asked abruptly.

"Groundhog Brummer," I said. "He can't help if he doesn't see his shadow."

"I'm not talking about him." Hambone's hand slammed against the top of my locker. "I'm talking about that groundhog I saw two days ago."

"Schnukums, are you sure you saw a groundhog in the school?" Luinda asked. I faked another sneeze. *Schnukums? Are you kidding me?*

"I saw it back on Wednesday over in the next hallway." Hambone pointed. "It was so fast. It rolled past me like a blur." Hambone buried his face in his hands. "After that, things turned ugly."

Something nudged my shoe. I looked down and saw Snow Cone's foot pressed against my heel. Something had definitely caught his attention.

"What is it?" I asked.

"Hey, where did he come from?" Hambone asked, jumping back in surprise. See, I told you Snow was good.

Snow Cone took a breath. "Rolled," he whispered.

"Rolled?" I repeated. "What do you mean ro—?" My finger instinctively shot into the air, and I spun back around to face Hambone. "Did you just say, rolled?"

"Yeah, it's not every day you see a groundhog shooting through the halls in a plastic ball."

My knees nearly buckled. "Where did you see it roll *to*?" I asked, trying to keep control of my voice. Sensing Snow Cone fidgeting next to me, I noticed him slowly removing his notebook and pencil from his backpack.

"Um, it went into the cafeteria and rolled under the milk cooler."

I nodded to Snow Cone, and though his legs were still positioned in a dancer's pose, he nodded in response. One of Twinkles's hamsters had been spotted. This was just the clue we needed to help us solve the mystery.

"That's good, Hambone." I ducked around his monstrous body and tiptoed backward until I was completely out of his swinging range. "We're going to get to the bottom of this. Believe me, you can count on us."

Hambone's massive chest heaved a sigh. "You better hope you do," he grumbled. "I don't like groundhogs."

Chapter 10

Clues in the Cafeteria

I sat down next to Snow Cone, Whiz, and Bubblegum at the lunch table and stared at my food. Ms. Borfish had called off sick for a third straight day, and the substitute cafeteria ladies had whipped up something that actually smelled edible. But instead of digging into my meal, I just twiddled my fork with my fingers.

Snow Cone and I had spent the last few hours practically disassembling the milk cooler in search of Twinkles's hamsters, but we came up with nothing.

"I don't get it," Snow Cone said. "You'd think we would've found something under all those cartons of milk."

I smacked the table in frustration. "I need to think about something else for a minute. My head hurts."

Twinkles had given me three days to find his hamsters, and I was no closer than when I had started. Building a new tree house was not an option, but if Twinkles blew those bombs, there'd be no way to salvage my beloved hangout.

"So," Snow Cone said, spooning a heap of creamed corn into his mouth. "Why exactly were you at the school last night, Bubblegum?"

That was a really good question and one I had forgotten

to ask in all the excitement. Just because a handful of us knew how to sneak into the school didn't mean we should do it, unless there was an emergency. I looked sideways at Bulkins, and his shoulders drooped.

"Don't get mad, but since I'm moving away soon, I couldn't just leave my collection behind," he said.

"Your collection?" I asked.

Bubblegum plopped a garbage bag onto the table. The bag was chock-full of thousands of pieces of ABC gum. "Do you realize how long I've been collecting? Some of these pieces are practically antiques." Bubblegum rummaged in the bag for a few seconds and pulled out a piece of gum that was gray in color and covered in cobwebs. For all we knew, it could've been a spider egg. "Take this one for example." Bubblegum dusted off the cobwebs. "This was one of the very first pieces of gum I ever chewed at Pordunce." He held the piece close to his nose, and his nostrils widened. "Piña colada." He popped the piece of gum into his mouth and smiled.

I felt like gagging, but the thought of Bubblegum crouching beneath rows of desks, scraping off old pieces of gum with a chisel brought tears of joy to my eyes. That was the Bubblegum I knew and loved. The four of us started to laugh, and for just one brief moment, things were back to normal.

Four Hips, Gavin, and Measles approached the lunch table and sat down across from me. All three of them were wearing ridiculous smiles on their faces.

"Guess what?" Four Hips punched his straw into his milk. "Gavin figured it out." He reached over and grabbed a handful of my mashed potatoes off my tray.

"Figured what out?" Snow Cone asked, sliding his tray out of Four Hips's reach and covering his mashed potatoes with his hands.

"I've figured out who the ghost is," Gavin said.

The sound of clattering silverware filled the lunch room as Bubblegum, Snow Cone, and I dropped our forks in unison.

"Who the ghost *is*?" I leaned forward in suspense. "You mean who it *was* when it was still alive, right?"

"Oh, the ghost is very much alive, and, in fact, it's not a ghost at all." Gavin drummed his fingers against the table.

"All three of you know about this?" I asked, looking at Measles who was smiling but appeared somewhat cross-eyed.

"Oh, no, I don't know what they're talking about," Measles said. "But I have this new anti-itch cream that causes the muscles in my face to flare out. I can't stop smiling no matter what I do."

"Well, who is it?" Whiz asked.

Gavin's eyebrows rose. "You can probably figure it out on your own just by following the clues. Think about it: where did the ghost come from last night?"

"A graveyard?" Whiz guessed.

"The afterlife?" Bubblegum suggested.

"Piedmont, West Virginia!" said Joshua Socket who was sitting two tables over and having a completely different conversation with Piñata Gonzales.

"The cafeteria," Snow Cone said, snapping his fingers.

Gavin's grin widened. "That's right. The cafeteria. Now, where did the ghost go after it attacked our group?"

I could tell several of my friends were about to blurt out wrong answers, so I quickly said, "Into the bathroom."

Gavin nodded. "But not just any bathroom. The Forbidden Bathroom. Only one person could survive the smell of the Forbidden Bathroom."

"What are you talking about?" Whiz was standing on the table.

Gavin sat back in his chair. "All right, here's the final clue: Ms. Borfish has been home sick now for three days. The day she stopped showing up was the first day the ghost appeared."

"Ms. Borfish is the ghost?" Snow Cone's face lit up with amazement.

"Precisely," Gavin said as he mashed the buttons on his calculator in triumph.

Measles was still smiling, but his eyes looked on the verge of crying. "Oh, that's sad. No one told me Ms. Borfish died. And now she's come back to haunt the school?"

"No, Measles. She didn't die," I said, speaking slowly. "She's pretending to be sick and sneaking around the school disguised as a ghost. That's just the type of thing that woman would do."

"I bet she loved scaring us all last night," Snow Cone said, pounding his fist into his hand.

Ms. Borfish would stop at nothing to ruin my elementary school career. It had been that way ever since the first grade when, apparently, I'd disgraced her lunch room by barfing up all the hash browns I'd eaten to earn my nickname. After all these years, she had finally picked her moment to attack.

"Well, what do we do now?" Bubblegum's voice disrupted my thoughts. "Just because we know who the ghost is, we still have ourselves a big problem. How do we stop her from terrorizing the school?"

He had a point. Ms. Borfish was a dangerous woman. Her spatulas could cut through a watermelon with one mighty swing.

Snow Cone jotted down possibilities in his notebook. "Just thinking about her, hiding in her trailer, trying on different-colored sheets makes my skin crawl. We need proof."

My eyes lit up. "That's it, Snow! Her trailer gives her

access to the school at any time during the day. That's how she knew when Bubblegum was in the school. If we time our attack, we can catch her in the act as she's changing into her costume."

"You want us to go into her trailer? Are you crazy?" Whiz asked. "That's like following a wounded rhinoceros into its cave, only Borfish isn't wounded."

"It'll be dangerous, and, to be honest, some of us might not make it back alive." I looked over at Measles. His anti-itch cream must've finally worn off because his smile had vanished.

Snow Cone stood up from his chair. "All we need are some photographs of her wearing her costume. That should be enough proof for Principal Herringtoe."

"Snow Cone, grab your camera," I said, pulling a tiny whistle out of my pocket and giving it a blow. Almost immediately, Pigeon hovered beside me in the air.

"Reporting for duty, sir!" Pigeon announced.

"Pigeon, I need you to send a message to the rest of the club."

"Yes, sir!"

"Tell them *the dish ran away with the spoon*."

Pigeon blinked. "Is that even possible, sir?"

"Pigeon," I started, but he was gone in a puff of feathers.

The lunchroom buzzed with excitement. We had a plan, we had a mission, and now we had a target. Ms. Borfish was going down.

"Boys," I said, fitting my backpack onto my shoulders and jabbing a pickle spear into my mouth. "Meet me out in front of the school tonight at eight o'clock and suit up in your paintball gear. We've got ourselves a ghost to catch!"

Chapter 11

A Bright White Flash

A brilliant yellow moon lit up the cloudless sky as I wiggled out of my bedroom window later that evening. I dropped my backpack over the side of the roof and shimmied down to the ground below. I was running a little behind and I knew Snow Cone and the rest of my pals were already stationed outside the school, awaiting my arrival. Gathering up my backpack in my arms, I gave a quick glance toward my tree house. The streetlight across from my yard had blown a bulb, but even in the darkness, I could make out the bulky shadows of the stink bombs plastered to the ladder.

I was about to leave when I noticed a small object resting by the base of the ladder, next to one of my mother's potted petunias. Upon closer inspection, I saw it was a paper sack with a note taped to the opening. Was this a message from Twinkles? Was he reminding me of the countdown to my tree house's destruction?

At first, I didn't recognize the handwriting, but when I saw the name at the bottom of the note, goose bumps poked up on my forearms. The message was from Melanie Thumbs.

Dear Hashbrown,

It was a brave thing you did the other night at the school. Thank you for saving Nugget's life from the Forbidden Bathroom. No one has ever done anything like that for him. I know you probably don't believe me, but I want us to be friends. Oh, stop smiling!

I immediately wiped the goofy grin from my lips and peered over my shoulder. *How did she know what I was doing in a letter?*

I shrugged and continued reading.

I heard you're going after the ghost tonight. Since I owe you one for saving Nugget, here's a bag of my special marbles. I'm giving you six of my best ones: two white flashers, two gray smokers, and two green slimers. Good luck, and no, I never cheated in our marble tournament.

Love,

Melanie

How about that? I bent over and snatched the sack of marbles from the ground. After all the mean things I said to her, I never would've thought she'd want to be my friend. I fished one of the marbles out of the bag and rolled it around with my fingers. Would they really work? If they did, they'd give me the edge in the battle with Borfish. But what if nothing happened when I threw one? Or worse, what if they did something terrible to me? Doubt filled my mind as I raised the marble up close to my ear and shook it. Something rattled inside. My marbles never rattled.

I scanned the yard. Just beyond the sidewalk, I found

my target—a small bush sprouting up next to a mailbox. I loaded the marble on my thumb, aimed, and fired.

The night lit up with a blinding white light, and I shielded my eyes from the painful flare.

Suddenly, the mailbox screamed. "Argh! Hashbrown! Why?" a voice shouted in agony.

"Who's there?" I demanded, rubbing my eyes with the backs of my hands.

The mailbox toppled over into the yard, and the small bush was yelping and trying to break free from its leash.

"Who do you think?" the mailbox asked.

As the light dimmed and I was able to see again, I discovered Camo Phillips rolling around by the sidewalk.

"Camo, what are you doing out here?" I asked, rushing over to his side. The little bush nipped at my ankles. "Ouch! Stop that!"

"I always walk my dog before bed," Camo said. "Why did you hit me with that ball of light? I thought you were my friend!"

"It was an accident. I didn't even see you standing there." That was one drawback to Camo's ability to blend in with any surrounding. His poor dog stumbled clumsily and almost fell off the curb into the road. It was amazing how Camo had been able to train his dog to disguise itself as a bush. Weird, but amazing.

Camo grumbled something under his breath and nudged past me, dragging his pet behind him with the leash.

"I'm really sorry," I called after him as he shrunk away into the darkness. "Holy cow!" I exclaimed, staring into Melanie's sack of marbles. "Now we're in business!"

Chapter **12**

Attack of the Slime Creature

The plan was set, but in order to catch Borfish in the act, we needed bait. Measles objected to the idea at first. Seriously, who wouldn't? Being tied up with a rope outside of the cafeteria, holding a barrel of Borfish's hash browns wasn't exactly safe, but it was the only way we could guarantee she'd be lured into action. And since Measles had been acting weirder than usual, my club unanimously picked him for the job.

We split up into two teams. Snow Cone and half of my squad accompanied Measles into the cafeteria while Whiz, Four Hips, Pigeon, and I staked out Ms. Borfish's trailer, ready to snap a picture of her in her phantom costume.

Crouching below the trailer window, we listened for the muted sounds of Borfish's favorite television channel, The Home Shopping Network. If my sources were correct, they were selling electric griddles on tonight's program. Ms. Borfish wouldn't miss it for the world.

Her trailer, however, was deathly quiet. Other than Four Hips munching on his Caesar salad, the property was silent.

"I knew it," I whispered, feeling the adrenaline pumping through my veins.

"What?" Whiz asked. His eyes flitted back and forth like two nervous fireflies.

"The only reason her television would be off right now is if she's up to something. I bet she's already sniffed out the bait."

"Should I send them a message, sir?" Pigeon asked. Pigeon had been clinging to my knee like a leech the entire time. I had almost forgotten he was still with us.

I shook my head.

"Please, sir!" Pigeon begged. "A warning! They need to be warned!"

"Pigeon, get off me!" I ordered, wiggling my leg to loosen his death grip. "There's no need for a warning because we're going to catch her in the act. That's what this is for, remember?" I shook Snow Cone's digital camera.

"So we're just going to snap a couple of pictures and that's it?" Four Hips asked. He had finished off his salad and was now tearing into his main course: pork chops and asparagus.

"How much food did you bring?" I asked.

Four Hips tucked his napkin under his chin and looked up in confusion. "Hey, I almost missed dinner tonight."

"Almost?" Whiz asked.

"Yeah, well, I didn't miss it, but I almost did. It makes me hungry just thinking about missing a meal." He sighed and poured a generous helping of gravy over his pork chops.

I rolled my eyes. "Look, it's not going to be a simple photo shoot. We've also got to locate and rescue Twinkles's two hamsters. If we don't, there's no point to any of this."

Ten minutes passed without a peep from inside the trailer. In his anxiousness, Whiz had literally destroyed Ms. Borfish's flower garden. I checked my watch. It was nearing nine o'clock and still no action. I knew for a fact she kept the barrels of hash browns under close surveillance. If just one potato was missing from her precious stash, she'd know.

"This isn't right," I whispered.

Whiz's eyes enlarged. "What if she's already in the school, sneaking up on the others?"

There'd been no messages from Snow Cone, but that was what we'd agreed upon—strict radio silence. We couldn't take the chance of our walkie-talkies blowing our cover. I glanced down at Pigeon, who was beginning to feel like a natural part of my leg as he cowered, attached to me like a baby possum. I snatched my walkie-talkie from my backpack. It was a risk, but if Whiz was right, the others could be sitting ducks.

"All right, be ready for anything." The four of us popped the safety switches off our paintball guns and steadied our fingers on the triggers. I pressed down the call button and signaled Snow Cone.

"Popsicle One, this is Big Tater. Over."

Soft fizzing followed as we waited, and then . . .

"Big Tater, I read you loud and clear. Over." Snow Cone's voice exploded out from my walkie-talkie. I had left the volume up too high. Cringing in fear, I twirled the volume knob down until the walkie clicked off. My eyes shot up to the window of the trailer and then back to the terrified faces of my friends.

"Do you think she heard that?" I asked.

The trailer door swung open with enough force to knock a half-eaten pork chop out of Four Hips's mouth. A hideous monster emerged from the shadows. The four of us screamed at the sight of Ms. Borfish. Her face was ghostly pale, covered in some sort of white paste, and her eyes were wild and on fire. She was wearing a bright purple bathrobe, and her hair was rolled so tightly in curlers, the paste smeared along her forehead was beginning to crack. She was the most frightening thing my eyes had ever seen.

Ms. Borfish roared, and with one massive hand, snatched Whiz off the ground like a rag doll. Struggling for freedom, Whiz lost the handle on his paintball gun, and it plummeted to the grass. Left with no other choice, Whiz did what he did best, but even this had little effect on the beast. She reached for Four Hips, who collapsed to the ground in a heap. Unable to lift his mass, she brought a bare foot down on his stomach so he couldn't roll away.

"What are you doing out here!" Borfish bellowed. Before I could react, she had me in her clutches. "Who are you?" she hissed.

The four of us were heavily camouflaged. I was wearing night vision goggles and a black beanie. But there was no way of knowing how long our camouflage would last.

I fired my paintball gun, but with one mighty chop, she snapped my weapon in two pieces, rendering it useless. Borfish wasn't supposed to catch us. I swung my arms and pleaded for my life.

"Please, let us go! We won't tell anyone your secret!"

Borfish cackled. She was sweating now, and the paste was streaming down the side of her face like a gooey waterfall. From this close, the mole above her lip looked like a snow capped mountain peak. Again, I tried to break free, this time swinging my legs as hard as I could. I felt a small weight lift off my knee and for a split second both Ms. Borfish and I were distracted as we watched tiny Pigeon flutter up over the trailer like a leaf caught in a breeze. Maybe I imagined it, but Pigeon looked relieved.

What would Borfish do with me? Most certainly I was headed back to Pordatraz, where I'd be peeling potatoes for the rest of eternity. Without proof of her disguised as the ghost, we were done for.

Proof! That's it! In all the commotion, I had forgotten about the camera. I fumbled with the strap and nearly dropped it.

"Now, let's see who I'm dealing with," Ms. Borfish said with a sinister chuckle.

SNAP, SNAP, SNAP!

I took three quick pictures right in her eyes. The flash blinded her, and she dropped me. Without a moment to lose, I fished one of Melanie's green marbles from the sack. Giving it a kiss for good luck, I pelted Borfish with the marble and a flood of green slime covered her from head to toe. She looked like a giant head of cabbage. Only the whites of her eyes were visible amid the slop.

The slime was thick and heavy and within seconds, it began to harden. Borfish fought, swinging her arms and legs. Whiz broke free from her grasp and Four Hips squirmed out from beneath her foot. There was a cracking sound, like the snapping of tree branches, and then we watched in disbelief as Ms. Borfish froze completely. Luckily she was still breathing inside her slimy statue.

I was exhausted, and apparently our struggle had worn out Ms. Borfish as well. Within a few moments, her eyes drooped closed and her growling was replaced by the sound of snoring.

I was dizzy and my hands shook, but we had stopped the ghost of Pordunce Elementary in her tracks, and now we had plenty of evidence to prove it. I slapped Whiz on the shoulder and gave Four Hips an encouraging nod.

"Start looking for those hamsters. They're bound to be around here somewhere." I searched along the ground and found my walkie-talkie. Turning it back on, I increased the volume and pressed the call button.

"Snow Cone," I said, still gasping for air. "We did it.

We've got her." Bringing down Ms. Borfish could quite possibly become my greatest victory.

The walkie squawked, and I pulled the receiver away from my ear.

"Hashbrown!" Snow Cone shrieked from the other end. "Where have you been?"

The urgency in Snow's voice surprised me. "I'm all right, Snow. I had to shut it off for a sec—"

"Hashbrown, the ghost! It's the ghost!" Snow Cone broke in before I could finish.

"Yeah, buddy. We got her," I said. "We caught Borfish in the act. She's not going anywhere." I winked at the others, and Whiz and Four Hips exchanged high-fives.

"Have you lost your mind?" Snow Cone shouted. "She's here!"

I smirked. "Yeah, I know, she's here. I mean, she's not *there*. She's out here by her trailer. You should see her. Melanie's green slimer marble is so cool! Borfish is completely—"

"Hashbrown, shut it!" I reared back from the walkie-talkie in alarm. Did my best friend just tell me to shut it? That was uncalled for. "Listen to me: Ms. Borfish is here in the school right now! That's what I've been trying to tell you. She came right out of the cafeteria and cornered us. We've got nowhere to run. We're trapped!" There was a pause in the conversation and then another voice, a strange, haunting voice that made my blood run cold, rose out of the walkie-talkie.

"You won't need that anymore, Snow Cone Jones."

The walkie-talkie fell deathly quiet.

Chapter **13**

Lies from Locker 366

"Snow Cone! Do you read me!" I shouted into my walkie-talkie as we cut across the playground and raced to the back entrance of the school. There was no answer.

"What are we gonna do?" Whiz asked. "We don't know how to catch a real-live ghost! Ms. Borfish was bad enough! Plus, it knew Snow Cone's name. How is that possible?"

I kept running at an all-out sprint. This was the second time in two days I'd sent my friends into danger. Last night, though I hated to admit it, Melanie had shown up just in time to save them. Now it was up to me. I stared down at the brown paper sack held tight in my fingers. I still had four special marbles left, and I was certain I would need them all.

We snuck through the secret passageway at the back of the school and stepped into a pitch-black hallway. Only then did we slow our speed to listen. Except for the sound of our own footsteps on the tile floor, the school was silent.

"Hashbrown!" Whiz said. "If we go after the ghost without a plan, we'll get caught like the others. We need help."

"There's no time!" I said. "We're on our own. There's no one else in the school to—" I snapped my fingers and tossed the sack of marbles to Four Hips, so I could rummage around in my backpack until I found what I was looking for. "Yes!" I exclaimed. "I know it's late, but we have no choice."

"What are you suggesting?" Whiz asked.

"Four Hips, you wouldn't happen to have any micro-waveable pizzas on hand would you?" I glanced at him.

"Maybe," Four Hips said. "Why?"

I held up one of my last Rip Strapinski baseball cards and smiled. "It's time we pay a visit to the Oracle."

After weaving our way through the school, we found the third-grade wing empty. Locker 366 towered above our heads like a coffin. Gabriel "The Oracle" Yucatan was the creepiest student in the school. Some fluke prank over seven years ago had landed him behind the door of locker 366. No fresh air. No field trips. And, as sad as it sounds, no recess. Needless to say, conversations with him tended to be a little tense. However, if one needed advice, one went to the Oracle. He knew about everything that was going on at the school.

I stepped forward and started the summoning ritual with six sharp knocks against the locker.

"Yes," a voice blurted from the locker. "What is it?"

"Um . . . uh . . ." The Oracle had surprised me. I hadn't expected him to answer so quickly, and with me barely beginning the ritual. Usually, you had to squeal like a pig, chant some ridiculous words, and cram your payment through the locker slot. That's why I'd brought my 2002 Rip Strapinski baseball card and Four Hips's microwaveable pizza.

"Uh, right. We've come to get your advice." I leaned forward and shoved the pizza and the baseball card through the slot. "This is for you."

"Oh, sweet!" the Oracle exclaimed. "Canadian Bacon." Next we heard the sound of the beeping on his microwave. "I'm starving," he said.

"Okay, well, can you help us?" I asked anxiously.

"Huh? Oh, sure. What do you want to know?"

I took a deep breath. "So you probably already know this, but my friends and I have been trying to get rid of a ghost here at Pordunce."

"Uh-huh, yeah, I read about that somewhere."

That was a weird thing to say. "Right. Anyway," I continued, "we think our friends have been captured by this ghost and we need to know what to do next."

"Ah, yes, I know exactly what you should do." There was a sudden fizzling sound and the Oracle erupted in a fit of hacking and coughing as black puffs of smoke billowed out of the locker slot. "Oh no! I burned it!" he shouted. "You're not supposed to leave the foil on, are you?"

Whiz and I stared at each other in disbelief. Did the Oracle just burn his pizza?

"You wouldn't happen to have another one would you?" the Oracle asked.

Four Hips shook his head. "No, that was the only pizza I had."

"How about another microwave?" There was the sound of him pounding buttons. "Crud! This one's toast."

I scratched the back of my head in confusion. "Are you okay?" I asked.

"Hang on a second," he said in between coughs. We listened as his footsteps tapered off, deep into the walls. After a few moments, he came running back, mumbling to himself under his breath as if reading the directions to something. "Hmmm. It says you pull this lever here . . ." Suddenly white foam sprayed out of the locker.

Whiz, Four Hips, and I sprang back into the center of the hallway to avoid the spray.

"What's gotten into him?" Whiz asked.

"I don't know. It's like he's a different person," I said.

Cautiously, the three of us approached the locker as the haze of foam dispersed. The Oracle was still talking to himself. After a few moments of loud hammering, he fell silent.

"Can you help us now?" I asked.

The Oracle screamed. "You scared me! Can't you see I'm busy?" he asked. "Where does he keep the paper towels?" The hammering sounds began again.

Did he just say "he"? I slammed my hand against the locker. "Who are you and what have you done with the Oracle?"

The hammering stopped. "I don't know what you're talking about," the Oracle said. "I am the Oracle."

"No you're not," Whiz piped in. "The Oracle never burns his pizzas."

"Sure I do. It was an accident. It happens all the time."

"Oh yeah, well if you're the Oracle, then you'll know the answer to this. What's Whiz's real name?" I folded my arms.

The Oracle chuckled. "That's easy. It's Whizley Mumfulson."

"That's not even my real last name, you dip," Whiz said.

"Give me another question," the Oracle insisted. "I'll prove to you I'm the real Oracle."

I thought for a moment. "Okay, why was Hambone trying to kill me a couple months ago?"

"Simple. You called him a ninny and ate all of his pretzels one winter evening."

I ran my fingers through my hair in disbelief. "What's going on at this school? How long have you been in there, pretending you're the Oracle?"

"Five years, thank you very much. It was right after that no-good Polly Perduka hit me upside the head with a Frisbee."

"Who is this guy?" Whiz asked.

I had no idea, but everything he said was a complete lie.

"Wait just a minute," I said, wagging my finger at the locker. "What were you doing last summer right before school started for the year?"

"Well, if you must know," the Oracle whispered. "I was on a special mission for the Queen. It involved two Hungarian crocodiles and a bearded woman named Lily Sue."

Our eyes widened, and the three of us shouted in unison. "FIBBER? What are you doing in the Oracle's locker?"

I should've figured it out sooner. Fibber is the world's worst liar and has been for as long as I've known him.

"I'm not Fibber," Fibber said. "I'm the Oracle."

"How did you get in there?" Four Hips stood on his tippy toes, trying to see through the locker slot.

"I was born in here," Fibber lied.

Whiz clapped his hands. "Remember? Hambone shoved Fibber into a locker a couple of days ago. He must've found a way through all the tunnels."

I nodded. "Fibber, we don't have time for any more games. Listen to me very closely."

"Yes, my son," Fibber said in a serious tone.

"We need to speak with the Oracle. So you're going to have to bring him here."

"Sorry, he's not here. It's just me." Fibber whistled. "Did you guys know he's got a disco ball in here? It's pretty amazing. I just wonder who he dances with."

"That doesn't make any sense," I said, rubbing my eyes in frustration. "If he's not in there, then where is he?"

A cold, bony hand seized my shoulder. "Well, well, well. If it isn't the infamous Hashbrown Winters."

I turned, and a tall, ghastly figure loomed over me. He was draped from head to toe in a white sheet with two slits cut out for his glowing red eyes.

Chapter 14

The Whistle and the Bug

"I bet you're surprised to see me," the real Oracle said.

I reared back against locker 366. "You're the ghost?"

The Oracle's red eyes flashed. "Yes, I'm afraid so."

"But . . . that's not possible," Whiz said.

The Oracle's body stiffened. "Oh, of course. Who'd ever expect to see the Oracle wandering the hallways, free to move about wherever he chooses? Oh no, not him. Because that poor schmoe is stuck in his locker and he's been there since before most of you were even enrolled at Pordunce."

"Well, yeah," I said. "But how did you get around the school? You were popping up all over the place."

The Oracle chuckled. "You didn't really think you were the only one who knew all of the secret passages at Pordunce, did you? I've known about them for years. I bet I even know a few you've never seen before."

"What are you talking about?"

"Oh, I don't know, like the trap door behind the milk cooler in the cafeteria or the hidden elevator beneath the desk in the abandoned classroom."

He was right. Those were new ones to me.

"How did you escape when we chased you into the

Forbidden Bathroom?" Whiz asked. "There's no way out."

"I guess you didn't know about the secret passageway behind the third stall's toilet."

"But how did you survive the smell?" Four Hips asked in wonder.

"What smell?" The Oracle's head tilted to one side.

"You didn't smell it?" I asked.

The Oracle waved a hand dismissively. "I may have noticed a faint odor in the air, but I've been trapped in my locker for seven years without the ability to take a bath. Believe me, I've smelled worse."

The three of us nodded in agreement. "So what now?"

"Now?" The Oracle's body straightened. "Now, you become my prisoners."

"But we didn't do anything." Four Hips's voice trembled.

"Oh no? You and your little friends rollick through these halls, going about your merry ways, never thinking twice about Gabriel Yucatan. Until the moment there's a bully or someone needs to know what's hidden in the meatloaf's special sauce. Then you run to me. You think you can just throw me a few treats, and I'll gladly tell you what you need to do. Then you leave, and all's well at Pordunce. Now it's my turn to rollick on the playground, and it's your turn to experience seven years in your lockers." The Oracle's shoulders quivered as he chuckled. "That's where your friends are right now. And once I find some impossibly strong padlocks, I'll seal you all up for good. Then, whenever I have a problem that's too hard for me to solve, I'll cram a pizza in *your* locker slots."

"But how? You've been trying to get out for years. How did you get out of your locker?" I asked.

"I owe my freedom to this," the Oracle said. The sheet covering his lanky body rippled, and his long, white fingers slipped out from beneath it, holding a tiny, silver whistle.

"It's like yours, Hashbrown. Only instead of Pigeon, this whistle brings other things to me."

I squinted, unable to recognize the object at first, but after closer inspection . . . "Is that a dog whistle?"

"That's right. A few days ago, some foolish second-grader shoved it into my locker, not knowing what would happen if I blew it." The Oracle threw his head back and laughed.

Whiz squirmed, and the sound of dribbling rose from his feet. "How could a dog whistle help you out of your locker?"

"Well, that night I was wandering the caverns of the school—as I often do after everyone leaves—when I happened to overhear Twinkles Marlow teaching his pets some tricks. Thinking it would be fun to tease the old geezer, I decided to play a few notes on my new whistle. The result was amazing." The Oracle brought the whistle back under his sheet and played an almost inaudible high-pitched note.

Several moments passed in silence, but then, from around the corner, two plastic balls appeared, driven by Twinkles's furry hamsters.

"You see, it was because of them that I was released from my tomb." The hamsters rolled all the way to the Oracle's feet, and he bent over to pluck them from off the ground. "This whistle forces them to come to me. I had no way of knowing that the wall I was standing behind had grown so old that the force of two rolling hamsters would send it crumbling to the ground. Hmmm, lucky me."

A fluke accident had freed the Oracle. I wanted to be happy for the guy. After all, if anyone deserved a chance at freedom, it was him. Still, he was handling this all wrong.

"Now, back to business. The three of you will follow me to the fifth-grade wing. I want to introduce you to your new homes." The Oracle's long arms stretched out before us, preventing our escape.

"Please, Gabriel, you don't have to do this," I begged.

A loud explosion sounded out from somewhere on the other side of the school. The four of us turned our heads to look for the source of the noise.

"What was that?" the Oracle asked. "Is this another one of your club members showing up for the party?"

It wasn't one of my people. Other than Pigeon, who couldn't make a noise like that if his life depended on it, my friends were all accounted for—most were stuck in lockers.

We listened closely and heard the patter of tiny feet against the floor. The sound grew louder, and after a few beats, something small and black scampered into view at the end of the hallway, down by the vending machines. From this distance, it looked about the same size as a small cat. The creature zigzagged all the way until it reached the edge of the lockers and stood three feet away from us.

"Ick, what is that?" the Oracle asked, bending over for a closer look.

"It's Phil!" I said.

The cockroach's antennae quivered excitedly.

"Phil?" Whiz asked. "You mean Hambone's pet, Phil?"

"Yeah, Phil can hear that whistling too," I explained. "It drives him crazy."

The Oracle clicked his tongue. "I had no idea my whistle would summon something so gross." He sighed solemnly. "Since I don't want it following me around . . ." He took a heavy step forward, bringing his foot down hard and just barely missing the cockroach as Phil darted out of the way.

Whiz scratched his head. "But how did Phil make that exploding sound?"

Four Hips patted our shoulders and pointed. "I don't think it was Phil."

We followed his finger, and all of us, including the

Oracle, screamed in surprise. Standing at the end of the hallway where Phil had appeared only moments before, was Hambone Oxcart. The man-child was panting. His giant body blocked our view of the vending machines, and even from this distance, he looked possessed.

"Who's been making that whistling sound?" Hambone roared.

"Oh, dear," the Oracle said, standing tall and rigid.

In four massive strides, Hambone lumbered forward, covering the distance in the hallway faster than a charging grizzly bear. There were dark circles etched around his eyes, and it looked like he hadn't slept much over the past few days. No doubt the Oracle's whistling had kept him and Phil awake. Hambone carefully picked Phil up in his hands and held him close to his ear. We watched wondrously as the insect whispered to Hambone.

"Oh . . . dear," the Oracle repeated, taking a small step back away from Hambone.

"He did *what*?" Hambone's eyes widened, and his head swiveled from side to side, releasing a series of loud cracks. Phil whispered into his ear again and, I kid you not, the cockroach pointed one tiny accusing paw toward the Oracle.

"Oh, my dear, that's not good." The last of the Oracle's words came out in a squeak.

Before any of us could blink, the Oracle took off like a rocket. He barely had time to round the corner before Hambone shot after him. The noise was tremendous, like the sound of stampeding cattle, and the force of Hambone's charge threw the three of us backward into the lockers.

Whiz was laughing. He was peeing as well, but mostly laughing. It was a miracle, but my thoughts turned to the Oracle. If the head bully of Pordunce was able to lay his hands on him, it was all over. No one stood a chance against

Hambone. But Hambone wasn't the smoothest cue ball on the pool table. If I had been able to survive his wrath, there was a really good chance the Oracle could get away too.

"Come on, guys, we've got to help him." I sprung up.

"Help who?" Whiz asked. "Hambone? Are you serious? I don't think he needs our help."

"The Oracle knows all of the secret passageways at Pordunce. He could get away. Plus, we still need those hamsters. Time is running out for our tree house!"

I opened my backpack and searched for a moment. Where were they? I'd used one of Melanie's marbles on Borfish, but now the rest were missing. Suddenly I remembered. "Four Hips, do you still have my sack of marbles."

Four Hips looked confused but he nodded as he handed back the paper sack. I took it, peered in the opening, and groaned. It was empty.

"Where are they?" I demanded, spinning around.

Four Hips belched out a puff of gray smoke.

"You ate them?"

"I'm sorry. I thought they were candy." Four Hips smiled sheepishly and burped again. This time a large green bubble floated out of his mouth. "They tasted awful."

"Then why did you eat them all?" Whiz asked. "You should've stopped."

Four Hips bowed his head in shame. "I thought they'd get better if I kept eating them." He looked up at me. "But they didn't. And that white one hurt my eyes."

I moaned in agony. "Four Hips!"

"I'm sorry, but I was hungry."

There was no point arguing about it anymore. We still needed to catch the Oracle. Did we have time to stop him before he vanished into the dark passageways of Pordunce? Or would we be forced to face his wrath on another day?

Chapter 15

Oh, Sweet Nuggets!

We found Hambone passed out and drooling with both of his thumbs crammed up his nostrils in the entryway of the Forbidden Bathroom. There was no sign of the Oracle.

"See, what did I tell you?" I said to the others as I dug my gas mask out of my backpack.

"You're not really going after him are you?" Whiz wore a look of astonishment on his face.

I adjusted the straps of my gas mask, pulling it tight over my head. "I don't have a choice."

"But Hashbrown, you don't even know where that passage leads. What if it's a trap?" Four Hips asked. Green slime still oozed out of his mouth, but at least the smoke had stopped.

"Look, someone's got to put a stop to this. I'm not just gonna sit around, waiting for Twinkles to pull the trigger."

The sound of footsteps halted our debate and much to our surprise, Melanie Thumbs and Nugget raced around the corner and joined us outside of the bathroom.

"What are you guys doing here?" I asked, actually relieved to see them.

"I picked up Snow Cone's message on my radio," Melanie said. "I would've come sooner, but Nugget made it to the fourteenth level of Scarecrow Apocalypse, and we had to wait until he could save."

"I've got priorities, man," Nugget said with a nod.

"What's going on?" Melanie nodded toward the door of the Forbidden Bathroom.

I took a deep breath. "It's a long story, but we found out the ghost is really the Oracle, and he's running amok throughout the school. If we don't catch him, Twinkles is gonna destroy my tree house with six stink bombs."

Nugget's eyebrows rose. "Who's Twinkles?"

"No time to explain, but this gets worse. The Oracle's trapped most of my friends in their lockers, and he won't stop until he's locked all of us up. Now I've got to chase after him through a secret passageway in the Forbidden Bathroom and put a stop to this madness once and for all."

Melanie puffed out her cheeks. "That's quite a story." She glanced down at Nugget. "Okay, we're coming with you."

"What?" I asked.

"What?" asked Whiz and Four Hips.

Melanie reached into her own backpack and brought out two gas masks. She tossed one to Nugget. "We owe you from the other night. Do you have any of those marbles left?"

I couldn't believe what she was saying. "Uh . . . no, we used them all." I gave Four Hips a withering look.

Melanie rubbed her hands together. "That's all right. I brought some extras."

"Okay, but I've got to know where you get them from. They're awesome!" I said.

Melanie smiled. "I told you. They're family heirlooms."

"Really?"

"Well, not exactly." She pulled a strand of hair out of her eyes. "I guess I kind of make them myself."

"You *make* them?" Four Hips asked.

"Yeah. At my last school I earned the highest grades in science and chemistry. I guess I just love mixing things together."

Whiz grinned. "Hey, Hashbrown stinks at science. Maybe you could be his tutor." He started to giggle but swallowed harshly when he noticed the look in my eyes. "Or maybe not," he muttered.

I quickly brought the gas mask down over my face to hide my embarrassment. Melanie's cheeks turned red and she too hid behind her mask.

"You know, I . . . I *could* help if you really . . . um, need it," she said, her voice muffled by the mask.

"Let's just make it out of this school alive and in one piece," I said. "We can talk about that some other time."

She nodded and the three of us, Nugget included, pushed open the door of the bathroom.

The secret passageway in the Forbidden Bathroom led us through a long tunnel, lined with hundreds of wooden barrels. We didn't have time to inspect them all but discovered most of them contained thousands of pounds of dried hash browns—Ms. Borfish's private stash. At the end of the tunnel, there was a doorway opening into the cafeteria. I held my finger up to signal Melanie and Nugget to keep quiet.

"Okay," I whispered. "Remember, being cooped up all these years has made the Oracle very dangerous. How many marbles do you have?"

Melanie pulled out a velvet bag and undid the drawstring. Inside were four marbles—one of each color of her special marbles plus her bull basher. I took hold of a green one and as quietly as I could manage, peered through the opening.

The cafeteria looked empty, but as I stepped through, a plastic ball whizzed by my foot. I yelled out in shock as another ball struck my ankle and I toppled to the ground. I dropped the marble and a wall of goo shot out across the cafeteria floor, glimmering like a sea of spinach.

The Oracle stepped out from behind the milk cooler

"You really thought you'd chase me down?" He flung his head back, and the empty cafeteria filled with his laughter.

Thick smoke from a gray marble billowed out of the opening behind me, and Melanie barrel-rolled into action.

"Whoa, what's this?" the Oracle asked. "Why, if it isn't Melanie 'Thumbs' Nottingham, who recently transferred here from Corked Elementary." The Oracle chuckled. "Oh yes, I know who you are, *and* I know how you win marble tournaments." He leaned forward and held his hand next to his face. "But we won't call it cheating, now will we?"

Melanie squealed. "I didn't cheat!" She took aim at the Oracle with her bull basher. "Give up, or else."

"I think not!" the Oracle fired back. A high-pitched whistle rang out from beneath his sheet, and the hamsters shot forward with unnatural speed, rolling together in a perfect figure-eight and catapulting right at Melanie. She only had time for one shot, and the first hamster took a direct hit, flying off course and into an empty trashcan, where its ball erupted with a barrage of angry squeaks. Melanie tossed her last special marble at the second hamster. It was a white flasher, and the cafeteria lit up with blinding light. I couldn't see a thing—none of us could, not even the hamster. Unfortunately, it never stopped rolling and struck one of Melanie's shins dead on. She fell to the ground in pain.

"You fools! You're no match for my brilliance," the Oracle bellowed. "For seven years I've waited for this moment of freedom. You didn't really think you'd stop me, did you?"

I scanned the floor, desperate for some kind of weapon, but all of our ammunition was spent. No more marbles. No more tricks. My eyes fell upon Nugget, still cowering in the entryway of the tunnel.

"Nugget," I gasped, "please, help."

Nugget shook his head. "What am I supposed to do?" he whispered. "I don't have any marbles."

The Oracle leaned out from behind the milk cooler. "Who are you talking to?"

I honestly had no idea what Nugget *could* do to stop the Oracle. He was only in kindergarten, and the Oracle was probably old enough for college.

"Run," I whispered to Nugget. "It's okay. Run away and save yourself!"

Nugget looked confused. Shaking with fear, he took a step back into the tunnel.

By now the Oracle had covered the distance, and his bony hand shot out, seizing Nugget by the collar and pulling him out into the open.

"Hey, let me go!" Nugget demanded.

"Well, if it isn't Nathanial 'Nugget' Nottingham. What do you plan on doing? Don't tell me. You're going to bore me to death with your silly video game achievements."

Nugget's brow furrowed. "They're not silly."

"I've seen you in the hallways, tagging along behind your sister and trying to show everyone your high scores."

Nugget's eyes darkened, his face turning a slight shade of pink. "So?"

The Oracle stooped lower to speak to Nugget eye to eye. "No one cares about your stupid scores."

"That's not true!" Melanie shouted, still clutching her shin. "I care!"

The Oracle clucked his tongue. "Of course *you* do."

"So do I!" I propped myself up on my elbows and nodded reassuringly at Nugget.

"Pish posh, you do not." The Oracle waggled a finger and returned his attention to Nugget. "Tell me, what's the best score you've ever earned?"

Nugget blinked. "Earned on what?"

"I don't care. You're highest score, what was it?"

Nugget looked at his shoes for a moment. "I've scored three million points on Tipsy Topsy Pinball."

The Oracle became quiet for a moment, his head tilted to the side. "*You* play Tipsy Topsy Pinball?"

"All the time," Nugget said. "It's an old game, but it's one of my favorites."

"And you scored *three* million points?" The Oracle put a hand on his hip.

"Yep. Why?"

"*I* play Tipsy Topsy Pinball," the Oracle said.

"You do?" Nugget looked up at the towering fiend.

"Why is that so hard to believe? They had video games when I was first imprisoned."

"What's your highest score?" Nugget asked.

The Oracle's hand shot under his sheet, and it appeared as though he was nibbling on his nails. "It's not important."

"No, tell me," Nugget pressed.

"Ah . . . well . . . Don't lie to me! You've never scored three million points!"

"Sure he has," Melanie said. "I've seen his high score."

The Oracle's head spun around to face us. "Three million points? I'm not a fool! Do you realize how impossible that is? You'd have to pass the twenty-fifth level in order to achieve a score that high."

Nugget giggled. "I've actually scored three million points at least a dozen times on that game. What's the big deal?"

The Oracle exhaled sharply. "The big deal? The big deal is that's the only game I've been able to play for the past seven years while trapped in my metal prison. It's the only one I own. And the highest total I've ever scored is two million points! So don't lie to me," he repeated.

"It's not a lie," Nugget said.

"Then prove it. Show me your scores." The Oracle folded his arms.

Nugget's hands immediately reached to his side but fell short. "I don't have my portable gamer anymore," he said, the pinkish color returning to his cheeks.

"HA!" the Oracle exclaimed. "I knew you were lying."

Nugget's hands shook. "It was broken the other night."

"A likely story." The Oracle pumped his fist in the air. "Unfortunately, without it, you have no proof."

"But I *did* have proof!" Nugget growled.

I watched as his eyes began to bulge and tiny red spots sprouted on his face. His whole body trembled. The Oracle was too busy celebrating to notice the change in Nugget.

"Nugget," Melanie said soothingly. "Just take it easy."

Nugget's bulging eyes looked up at his sister. He was trying to control his breathing, and I knew if he took a moment to relax, his fit of anger would go away.

I couldn't let that happen.

"Hey, Nugget?" I asked, snapping Nugget's attention onto me. "The Oracle's right."

Melanie gasped. "Hashbrown, don't say that."

I ignored her, and Nugget's body started shaking harder. "He's right," I repeated. "Without that game, you'll never be able to prove your high scores to anyone. And not just on pinball, but on all of your games."

"What are you doing?" Melanie slapped my arm. Nugget's eyes appeared ready to explode.

"All your scores have vanished. You have to start all over, and who knows how long it will take to beat them again. You would've been better off having never played those games. Your legacy is over. No more Nugget champion."

The Oracle took notice of our conversation. "Hashbrown, I don't think I understand what you're trying to do here."

I tuned out Melanie and the Oracle's voices and honed in completely on Nugget. He stepped toward me, his hands clenching and unclenching rapidly. This was a dangerous risk, but I had to hold out just a little longer. Nugget took another step and was now within striking distance. I've never seen such hatred, and it was all directed at me.

Wait for it. I said to myself. *Wait for it.*

"Nugget, I just have one last thing to say to you," I said in as calm a voice as I could manage.

Nugget's teeth chattered, and his lips puffed out. One more step and he would be on top of me.

"Everything you hold dear went up in smoke when your video game was broken, but aren't you forgetting something?" Nugget's hands stretched forward and closed around my throat. They were stronger than I expected.

"What's that?" Nugget's voice was not his own. It sounded like a demon.

I closed my eyes and nodded toward the Oracle. "He was the one that broke your video game. It was because of the Oracle that everything was destroyed."

For a brief moment, I was afraid I was too late and Nugget wouldn't hear my final words. Slowly Nugget's head pivoted almost one hundred and eighty degrees on his neck. He stared down the Oracle and fury blazed in his eyes.

"Oh . . . sweet . . . NUGGETS!"

Chapter 16

One Last Marble Match

I stood before a tower of cardboard boxes. They were labeled in black permanent marker with words like: "Bathroom" and "Odds and Ends." Snow Cone appeared in the doorway and stood next to me, staring at the depressing display of brown squares.

"Come on, Hashbrown," he said, patting me on my shoulder. He crossed the room, selected one of the boxes at the top of the stack, and heaved it onto his shoulder. "Bubblegum's van's almost full. If we don't hurry, we won't have time for pizza before he leaves."

I had hoped this day would never come. There had been so much excitement during the past two weeks that most of us had forgotten Bubblegum was going to move away.

You're probably wondering if things got back to normal. Well, it's hard to say.

My eyes have never seen a more awesome display of fighting skills than when Nugget swelled up and pulverized the Oracle. Eventually, Melanie and I had to drag Nugget off of him, and, after a long conversation, the Oracle decided to leave the school and move on to better things.

Gabriel Yucatan left Pordunce Elementary in peace. Where

he journeyed is a mystery, but some say he wandered off to live as a hermit in the wilderness. I plan to keep a supply of Rip Strapinski cards and microwaveable pizzas at the school on the off-chance he returns, but it seems unlikely he ever will.

In the meantime, Fibber Mckenzie has refused to leave the Oracle's locker. He says it's roomier than his own bedroom, and it makes the perfect place for him to lay low whenever he's done running spy missions for the Swedish government. He stays busy offering his own predictions, mostly to first and second graders. They don't make any sense because they're all lies, but Snow Cone and I stop by every day just to hear his voice.

Twinkles literally toe-tapped with joy when I returned Pepper and Siegfried to him. The next morning, he disarmed all of the stink bombs on my tree house and said we were even. We shook hands, and he even gave me the bombs as a peace offering. I'm not sure if they'll work or not, but the school musical, Puffy the Happy Blowfish, has its opening-night performance next weekend, which should be the perfect opportunity to test one out.

It turns out Ms. Borfish's illness starting on the same day the Oracle escaped from his locker was really just a coincidence. We were pretty worried she would recognize one of us as the culprits who attacked her, so it was a relief when she called off sick for another whole week. Of course, when Principal Herringtoe stuck up missing posters of Borfish all over the school, we decided it was time to send him an anonymous message about the growling, green statue outside her trailer. Now that she's back, she's been acting even weirder. Still, I don't think she has any clue it was us; although, I do find it suspicious how she gives me three extra helpings of hash browns whenever I walk through the lunch line.

Back to normal? Yeah, I guess things are as normal as

they can be at Pordunce.

I frowned and snagged a box. Immediately my hands were glued to the cardboard.

"What the?" I said, trying to pull my fingers away from the gooey substance.

"Oh, hey, I've been looking for that," Bubblegum said as he entered the room. "That's my last wad of Gooseberry gum. I chewed that for three weeks straight back in kinder-garten." Bubblegum pulled the sticky gum from my fingers and popped the pieces into his mouth. After smacking his lips for a few seconds, he smiled with satisfaction. "Good ole' Gooseberry. That was a really good year."

I gagged and wiped my hands against my jeans. Some things I could live without.

"Where's everyone else?" I asked. The house was pretty quiet.

"Most of them are outside already. Except for Pigeon. I haven't seen him since this morning."

"Really?" That wasn't like Pigeon. I pulled out my whistle and gave it a blow. One of the boxes midway up the tower quivered and toppled over. Pigeon rolled out, covered with old newspaper funnies and Styrofoam peanuts.

"Pigeon, what are you doing?" I asked, bending over and helping him to his feet.

"Oh, I don't know, I was just . . . just . . ." His eyes grew glassy and he started sniffling. Within seconds he was sob-bing. "I'm just going to miss Mr. Gum so much!" He buried his head under my arm.

"Who's Mr. Gum?" Bubblegum whispered.

"That would be you, Bubblegum," I said.

"Me? You're gonna miss me?" Bulkins asked.

"Of course, Mr. Gum. You have been a great mentor to me. What will I do without you?"

Bulkins popped a bubble and scratched his head in confusion. "I don't know what you're talking about. I stick gum in your hair almost every day."

"And I'll forever treasure your kindness," Pigeon said, bowing low.

"Right, well . . ." I stuffed a box filled with pillow cases into Pigeon's arms, and he nearly toppled over. "Come on, help us carry out these boxes before things get too awkward in here."

Outside, the whole gang stood around Bubblegum's van as his older brother, Kibbles, showed off his new cell phone.

"And you can walk around anywhere you want and still talk to people?" Measles asked, amazed by the phone. He reached out to touch the buttons, but Kibbles yanked it away.

"Yeah, Measles, it works like any other cell phone in the world. Where have you been for the last ten years?" Snow Cone asked.

Measles stood up straight, looking worried. "I don't remember!" he gasped. "Where *have* I been for the last ten years?"

Everyone groaned. Sometimes we just needed to ignore him.

Bubblegum and I shoved the last of the boxes into the back of the van and slammed the door shut. This was it. I never imagined this day would ever come. It wasn't how it was supposed to be. Snow Cone, Bubblegum, Measles, Four Hips, and Whiz were my original club house pals. We were legendary, and now one of the pillars was crumbling. We had grown so much since that fateful day in kindergarten, when the first boards were nailed to the tree in my backyard. Now there was Hummus, Yeti, Pigeon, Butter, Mensa, and Gavin in the group, and I'm certain there were dozens more to come in the future.

Someone cleared his throat, and I looked up to see Melanie

and Nugget standing a couple of steps away from the van.

"We heard there was pizza," Nugget mumbled. "And I wanted some." He held a new video game console in his hands, and the lights of Tipsy Topsy Pinball lit up his face.

I smiled, and Melanie gave me a wink.

"You know, it's not like I'm moving out of the state," Bubblegum said, kicking a rock with his shoe. "I'll be in another school, but I'll still be here for sleepovers and stuff."

He was right. Corked Elementary wasn't the worst place he could go. It was only forty-five miles away. We could be at his place in less than an hour in my mom's van. And we could get there even faster if we used Mashimoto's jet pack.

Bubblegum's mom appeared in the front door. "Eric, your father's running a little late."

Bubblegum cringed. "That's not my name, Mom, but thanks for letting me know." We all chuckled.

His mom folded her arms. "What I meant was that you all have an hour or two to hang out before we leave. Should I call for pizza now, or is there something else you and your friends want to do?"

A light breeze nipped around our ankles. It sure did smell like spring in the air, and the weather was perfect. There were dozens of things we could do in an hour or two. We hadn't played paintball in awhile, and with weather like this, a water balloon war wasn't entirely out of the question.

"You know," Melanie said, gaining the group's attention. "The playground at Pordunce is empty right now."

"Well, no duh—it's a Saturday," I said.

Melanie rolled her eyes. "That would mean the marble arena is empty as well."

A murmur rose up amid my friends, and all eyes fell on me. I rolled my shoulders. "I hear you. Are you suggesting a little rematch?" I asked.

Melanie nodded. "If you're up to it. We could keep it simple. Just for fun. An exhibition, or—"

"Or we could put your trophy on the line. That is, if you're not scared of losing it." I nudged Snow Cone with my elbow.

Melanie's eyes narrowed. "Oh, I'm not scared."

"Then a tournament?" I looked around the group, and everyone nodded.

Melanie licked her lips. "That sounds good, but what are you going to play with? Do you need to borrow one of my bull bashers for the match?" She rolled her skull marble around in her hand.

"Nah," I said, shaking my head. I dug into my pocket and pulled out my own blue and white bull basher.

Pigeon's eyes brightened. "How did you get that back?"

"Yeah," Snow Cone chimed in. "Last time I saw that, it was on display in the first-grade wing."

"It wasn't easy, Snow. And I'm afraid our Spring Seminar will be a little crowded this year with all the free passes I handed out in order buy this puppy back." I tossed the bull basher in the air and caught it. The marble had a dusting of cat litter on it and it smelled funky, but it would still shoot true.

"We can keep the match simple. You know, low key," I said to Melanie.

"I agree. We have enough witnesses here to prove the winner," Melanie said. "It doesn't need to be big."

"Uh-huh," I said and then turned to face Snow Cone. "Snow, alert the media. Bring the whole stinking town if you have to."

Snow Cone nodded. "I'm on it."

"Bubblegum." I patted Bulkins on the shoulder. "This one's for you."

Snow Cone's Map of
Pordunce Elementary

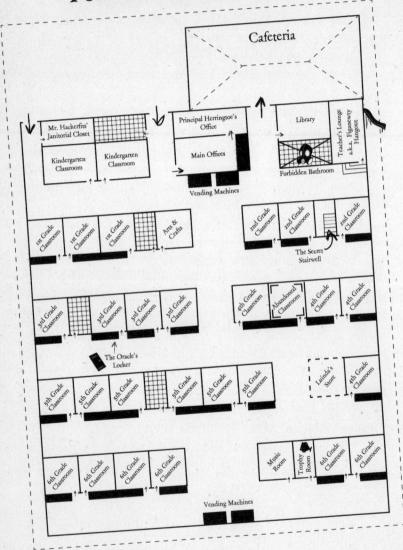

Discussion Questions

1. Hashbrown is hit with some tragic news when he learns his good buddy Bubblegum is going to move away. Have you ever had a good friend move to another school? How did you work to keep your friendship close?

2. What if it was up to you to solve the mystery behind a phantom haunting your school? What tools would you use to look for clues?

3. In what part of the story do you think Hashbrown showed the greatest amount of bravery? Has there ever been a time when you needed to show courage, even though you were afraid?

4. If you could visit just one location in Pordunce Elementary, where would you go and why? Would you go alone or take your best friend?

5. Nathanial "Nugget" Nottingham was a character created by a real elementary school student named Kaitlyn Larkin. If you could create a character for the Hashbrown adventures, what would your character's name be and what would he or she look like? To print out your own Create-a-Character sheet, ask a parent's permission and then go to www.hashbrownwinters.com.

About the Author

Frank L. Cole was born in a quiet town in Kentucky where he spent most of his childhood sharing exaggerated stories for show and tell. He now lives in Utah with his wife and three children.

If you want to read more about Hashbrown, check out *The Adventures of Hashbrown Winters* and *Hashbrown Winters and the Mashimoto Madness*. And be sure to look for Frank's newest title: *The Guardians of the Tebah Stick*, coming March 2011.

You can also visit Frank online at:
franklewiscole@blogspot.com
and www.hashbrownwinters.com.